Manhandled
Black Females

Victoria King

"TO SOW THE FALLOW SOIL"

PENNYWELL DRIVE . P.O. BOX 90883 . NASHVILLE, TENNESSEE 37209

WINSTON-DEREK
Publishers, Inc.

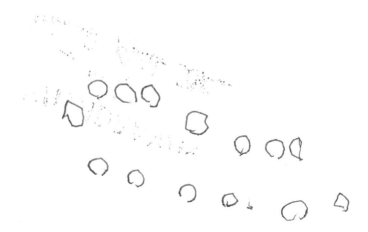

PUBLISHED BY WINSTON-DEREK PUBLISHERS, INC.
Nashville, Tennessee 37205

Library of Congress Catalog Card No: 91-66854
ISBN: 1-55523-478-X

Printed in the United States of America

With deepest gratitude to Professor Alison Anderson, Professor Kimberle Crenshaw, and Professor Christine Littleton, none of whom have seen this manuscript but all of whom encouraged me to listen to my own voice.

Special thanks to Professor Bryan K. Fair, a truly special brother who was a beacon in many law students' lives.

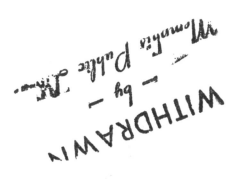

Contents

Introduction

nitially when I began writing this manuscript, I was so enraged at the character assassination of the black female by *The Black Man's Guide to Understanding the Black Women* and the black community's response to that book (the author claims to have sold over 200,000 copies of the book) that all I could think about was ramming the book down Shahrazad Ali's throat. Yes, black women, like most normal people, do get angry. We have much to be angry about. However, in the process of writing this manuscript, which is actually a semi-historical, -social, -legal, and -political analysis of the problems affecting black relationships and not just a putdown of Mrs. Ali's book, I was forced to clear my mind and come to grips with what was really bothering me—the hateful barbs that historically have been directed toward black women in America. Mrs. Ali's book is just the icing on the cake.

Most blacks are well acquainted with the reputed legendary loud-talking, over-sexed, sassy, promiscuous black female called Sapphire, whose favorite pasttimes are reputed to be spending money and getting on some brother's case. Comedians like Eddie Murphy, Richard Pryor, Flip Wilson, and Redd Foxx have made a fortune berating Sapphire. This image of Sapphire was created long before the author of the *Black Man's Guide* put the insults into print for the world to behold. In fact, "Sapphire" was the name of the loud and sassy black woman in the television comedy "Amos 'N Andy," who was regularly seen fussing and fighting with her husband, Kingfish. Any American, whether black or white, six or sixty, who has watched the nightly parade of sassy black maids, scantily-clad black female undercover cops, and black prostitutes on television is also well acquainted with the image of Sapphire, if not the name.

Because of the pervasiveness of the Sapphire image in both the black and white communities, one need not have read books like the *Black Man's Guide* to understand what the Sapphire image is about. The story is always the same—whether her mouth is too big or her skirt too short, the utterly deviant black female creates chaos wherever she goes. The image of black females' promiscuity was created during the slavery era to justify the sexual exploitation of black women and the need for white male domination. Through the centuries, the image has grown to encompass every aspect of black females' personae. Now, however, the negative Sapphire image is used by many to justify the need for black male domination.

Because so many of the negative Sapphire images are catalogued in the Black Man's Guide, I frequently direct my comments to that book. However, the reader need not have read that book to understand my comments. One need only look around and think about the image of black women in the popular media.

As distasteful as I found Mrs. Ali's overarching theme—that because the black man is a god-like creature who is genetically superior to the lazy, unclean, foul-mouthed, savage and animal-like black female, who spends all her time plotting against him, the black male is thereby entitled to beat the black woman into submission—I hold no grudge against Mrs. Ali. I feel sorry for her. Though many label her the perpetrator of confusion, she is not a perpetrator, she is a victim. Like millions of other black Americans, she is a victim of the American system of racial oppression that is so brutal, repressive and dehumanizing that the victims learn not only to hate themselves, but also to beat themselves unmercifully long after the master is dead.

Black people in America are not just like white people except a different color. Black people are not just like any other immigrant group that landed on the shores of America. Black people in America are the victims of hundreds of years of ruthless, brutal, institutionalized, soul-killing and mind-destroying, racist and sexist terrorism and oppression. I blame the government of the United States for the self-hatred that has been engendered in black people in America. One cannot enslave an entire race of people, subject them to unspeakable oppression, terrorism, horror, brutality and degradation for more than 200 years and then one day say "So, we made a little mistake—you're free now," and not expect monumental tragedy to result. Mrs. Ali's book is merely a symptom of the tragic dehumanization of black people that began with the docking of the first slave ship in America. The tentacles of oppression continue to reach into the future and claim victims.

Judging from the favorable response it has received, Mrs. Ali's book probably could have been written by any of many black people in America. These people are not lunatics. They are our friends, family, lovers, and next-door neighbors. That is the horror of Mrs. Ali's book! That is what makes me break into a cold sweat and keeps me awake at night. Perhaps we should thank her for bringing up a subject we sorely need to deal with, however unpleasant.

Someone must reach out to those who identify with the vile hatred and bitterness propagated by the Black Man's Guide, and show these people the error of their thinking. Though in the particular case of the Black Man's Guide the hatred is propagated by a black woman, this hatred is the same hatred that has been propagated against blacks by American society-at-large for centuries. If we burn or ban the book or refuse to talk about it in hopes that it will go away, we deceive only ourselves. The problem is not that the words were printed on paper but that the ideas already existed in the hearts and minds of men and women in America, both black and white. Mrs. Ali only expressed the hatred that many others feel but are afraid to acknowledge in other than surreptitious ways. Reasonable people may disagree on many issues, but when the reasoning process is abandoned altogether, danger lurks.

Rather than merely downgrading Mrs. Ali's book, or offering a barrage of boring statistics that can be interpreted 10 different ways by 10 different people, I offer what I know best—my own life experience. I was raised in the South as one of 8 children; enrolled in a Midwest college where I met and married an All-American football player who is the father of my 15-year-old son; divorced, served an apprenticeship with the International Brotherhood of Electrical Workers and became a journeyman electrician; obtained an undergraduate degree in economics at Fordham University, summa cum laude; quit the electrical trade to attend law school 2 years after being beaten up and raped on a construction site in New York City. I am currently in my last semester of law school at UCLA. Hopefully by the time of this book I will be a practicing attorney.

I do not present a string of credentials to dazzle the minds of the young people I hope will read this book and think seriously about black male/black female relationships. Instead, I wish to impress upon young men and women that I am no different than the people one passes on the streets everyday except that I survived where others less fortunate have perished. Underneath the veneer, I am the same poor black girl from Texas that I was in my youth, except that I tired of being kicked around and learned how to stand up for myself. I am willing to share some of my most painful experiences in life in hopes that one less black woman in America will fall into the traps I fell into or be subjected to the abuse I faced.

Writing this book was a catharsis for me. Many nights I sat at my computer in tears trying to make words express the agony and rage I feel at the way in which black women in this country are pushed aside like a worthless pile of rags. Though at age 40 I am no longer searching for a black man, I cannot turn my eyes from the many young black women I know are desperately searching and find only disappointment and heartbreak. I have known so many warm and caring black women that deserve better treatment than we customarily receive.

I would like to invite Shahrazad Ali to my home and introduce her to some of my black female friends to show her how wrong she is about the intentions of black women. We do not exist solely to make life miserable for black men and were hurt deeply by her unfounded accusations and the hateful barbs she directed at us in her book. The very young black women who are trying so hard to establish meaningful relationships with black men were particularly maligned. I hope that even those who disagree with my analysis of the problems facing blacks in America, will at least consider a different perspective. As a 40-year-old black female who has paid her dues, I have much to say about the plight of my black sisters in America. Please, have a seat and listen for a while.

Victoria King, alias *Sapphire*

Chapter 1

Reflections on Childhood

Early in life I learned that society makes acute distinctions between black people and white people, as well as acute distinctions between men and women. In my youth, few of these distinctions made much sense to me. Fortunately, youth is merciful and though I sensed that something about these lessons did not ring true, I did not realize the significance of these lessons until later in life.

My first lesson on the differences between black people and white people occurred on the first and only train ride that I can remember from my youth. I was 3 or 4 years old at the time and had just gotten a brand new, double-breasted, brown and green hound's-tooth coat. It was the most beautiful thing I had ever seen and I was quite proud to wear it. I remember hearing my parents whispering something about the "colored" section and thinking that we had a special place. I was too young to realize the stigma that was attached to being "colored" and having a special place on not only public accommodations but in life in general.

My first lesson on the differences between men and women came shortly after the lesson on being black. I was quite fond of following my father around the old farm on which we lived until I was 3 or 4 years old. He did not seem particularly distressed by my habit until the day that I followed him quite far from the house and he had not realized that I was following him from a distance. When I realized that I could not cross over the barbed-wire fence like I had watched my father cross, I called out to him to come back and help me. Alarmed at the sound of my voice, he raced back to the fence, jerked my doll away from me and bawled me out for following him. When I started to cry and protested that I wanted to go into the woods with him, he shouted that the woods were not for girls and that I could never go there. From now on, he scolded, I would have to learn to stay in the house with my mother. My place was there. In a huff, and all the while lecturing me on not being a tomboy, he marched me back to the house and delivered me to my mother's arms. I was too young to realize the limits attached to being female or I would have cried much harder.

Through the years, I have learned the lessons of being black and of being female quite well, usually because I have learned the hard way. Living in a world where there is one set of rules for blacks and another set for whites, and where there is one set of rules for women and another set for men can be a contradictory and confusing experience for those who are the least powerful in both realms, black females. Many black females who do not learn to live with the contradiction perish. Many black females who do learn to live with the contradiction survive, but not without scars. For the most part, our stories are told only to each other because those outside our realm are uncomfortable with our stories. To those outside the realm of black women, we appear strange and angry or hostile. We are labelled Sapphires.

Because of the dearth of information about black women, myths and legends are frequently spawned to explain who and what we are. Unfortunately, most of these myths are inaccurate. No doubt the first myths were born the day the first slave ship docked in America. The black-skinned men and women with kinky hair who arose from the stinking hulks of the slave ships must have been a sight to behold for whites, who were accustomed to describing the world with themselves as the source and reference point of all being. How could this blackness come from whiteness?

And so stories were created to maintain whiteness as the center of being and of all that was good. It is not surprising that in a society where white women, who dared to be different or defy authority were burned at the stake as witches, that blacks would be viewed as devils incarnate. The black she-devil was saved from being burned at the stake because she had great economic worth as a breeder and a laborer.

Conveniently for my purposes, the *Black Man's Guide to Understanding the Black Woman*[1] chronicled a number of the myths that exist in society-at-large about black women. An examination of these myths reveals how and why the black community and society as a whole have perpetuated myths about black women. Most of what was written in the Black Man's Guide was not new. The notions that black women are pushy and aggressive, unclean, promiscuous, and hard to get along with are not new. Most of what was written was merely a repetition of the myths surrounding black women that one hears everyday, except that the language used to describe black women was more vicious than usual. These myths attach themselves to innocent black girls in their youths and follow them to the grave. Where once these myths were used to explain the problems in the slave quarters (that required the nightly presence of many masters), now these myths are used to explain the problems in the black home or in black male/black female relationships. As always, the analyses reveal that the problem is the treacherous black she-devil.

On reading the slanted and superficial analysis of the problems between the black man and the black woman in the *Black Man's Guide to Understanding the Black Woman*, I was forced to conclude either that I was not raised in America or that the history of millions of black women like myself was once again being distorted. My childhood was

2

not spent sitting under my mother's feet, listening to her and her friends talking about my father or any other black man, and learning how to "scam" on the black man. Neither do I "act up" because I want a strong black man to discipline me (discipline all too often meaning to put a few knots on someone's head). I am not so vain as to think there is some magic power in my love that can solve all of the black man's problems and enable him to cast off his shackles and rise to greatness, or so short-sighted as to suggest we shall overcome by producing more babies than "Whitey."

On my first cursory examination of the *Black Man's Guide*, I was not sure whether I should laugh or cry. "Surely this is a joke," I thought, as I pinched myself to make sure I was not having a bad dream. The one thing I was sure of was that the book did not represent my life experience as a black woman.

Unfortunately, I have grown accustomed to feeling misrepresented in the world in which I live. When confronted with any so-called "objective" analysis, I am chronically confused by the use of the words "we," "blacks," and "women." Mentally, I must pause to figure out which "we" or "blacks" or "women" the speaker or writer means and where, or if, I fit. When society speaks of "we," it speaks of the white male's experience. When society speaks of "blacks," it speaks of the black male's experience. When society speaks of "women," it speaks of the white female's experience. From the perspective of those whose identity and life experience are thereby summarily dismissed by these "objective" analyses, these analyses are subjective indeed.

The speaker and those of his class are never disturbed by the dismissal of the experiences and perspectives of others because the speaker is generally quite ignorant of what these different experiences are. Indeed, it is difficult to miss what one has never known. The speaker just assumes that the only important perspective is his own—the white male experience, or her own—the white female experience. Most distressing are the black men who just assume that the only important perspective of the black race is their own—the black male experience. The black female and her experiences are dismissed as irrelevant in every single one of these categories as if she did not exist.

Although society will readily concede that there is a black culture, white society is loathe to admit that there is a white experience or white culture. It would be dangerous for white society to acknowledge the existence of a white culture as scholars would no doubt seek to define this culture and the results would be distressing to many, both black and white. Open acknowledgement of the white culture would destroy the myth of equal opportunity. If white society were to admit that there is a white culture, then white society would also have to admit that what we consider "the norm" is simply the culture that is learned and perpetuated in white homes—not some absolute moral truth or standard descended from the heavens above. While "objective" analyses may give the appearance of neutrality, the appearance of neutrality is simply the illusion by which the traditional perspective is made to appear ordinary and beyond question. Though to many the world appears to be an unmediated reflection of "what is," it is instead at every stage made and not found.

If white society were to suddenly acknowledge the existence of a white culture, most embarrassing to white society would be the fact that the only group of white Americans who has been honest enough to readily acknowledge the existence and operation of the white culture and who have fought hard to defend their version of this culture are the redneck southern segregationists and white supremacists, not the "genteel" lords and ladies of the mansions who directed others to do their dirty work, but the common class of white men and women who took the streets with bricks, bottles, fists, ropes, and guns to maintain segregation, i.e., American apartheid. So, to distance themselves from this group, many whites continue to deny that a white culture exists. Instead, they insist that neutral values prevail and that all who participate in this neutral value system have equal advantage.

As members of the white culture, the common class of whites was all too familiar with the operation of the white culture and its economic value system. Those at the bottom of the white culture knew their place well and were smart enough to figure out that since they were at the bottom, their economic advantages would be the first to be sacrificed when "equality" had to be financed. Uncle Sam never forgets to send the tax bill and the penalty for nonpayment is harsh. These white men and women had played by the rules and were not about to have the rules of the game changed on them in midstream. They were prepared to crucify blacks and whoever else got in the way in order to protect their position in the hierarchy of white American culture for this position had allowed them to enjoy distinct economic advantages. If not for their racist ideology, these white men and women could almost be pitied. It is never easy to fall from one's rung on the ladder.

It would be dangerous for white America to acknowledge that there is a white culture because such acknowledgement is to admit that in spite of the propaganda in the Constitution (a document so craftily written that the word slavery is never even used and yet by the Constitution blacks were enslaved), there are distinct racial interests at stake and in conflict in America. These racial interests are divergent, not convergent. The race with the upper hand will almost always be able to promote its interests to the detriment of others. Many of these

4

others do not realize the interests of their race are compromised daily as they have bought into the melting pot theory. Thus dominant white males are enabled to continually perpetuate the interests of the white race.

These men are not about to acknowledge that there is a white culture, just as there is a black culture or a Vietnamese culture, because once the white culture is acknowledged we will no longer be able to operate under the delusion of a color blind society and will be forced to admit that by its very nature, politics is a racial animal—always has been, always will be. That race should therefore be taken account of in our system of politics or that the system should be adjusted to provide for proportional racial representation to remedy the racial politics that have always existed (to the detriment of nonwhite minorities) and will always exist is a disturbing thought to those who have reaped the benefits, to those who continue to reap the benefits, and to those who leave this world knowing that their heirs will continue to reap the benefits. Therefore the political system and concomitant legal system continue to promote the propaganda that "we" are one monolithic system with a singular interest as opposed to the divergent interests that those without blinders or rose-colored glasses can well see.

White males encourage white females to believe that their interests are the same as the white males', just as black males encourage black females to believe that their interests are the same as the black males'. In this system the dominant males of both races, with their loyal troops behind them, can continue to fight for a bigger slice of the pie. The rest of us must be content to eat from these men's tables. And so, the "objective" analyses that are really quite subjective, depending on the category into which one falls, continue. These "objective" analyses continue to blind us to reality, lest some of us, like Gulliver, arise from a deep sleep and shake the very foundations of the king's empire.

Therefore, as if the black woman were invisible, irrelevant or nonexistent, society continues to speak of the white male experience when it speaks of "we," the black male experience when it speaks of "blacks," and the white female experience when it speaks of "women". Thus the interests of whites continue to be promoted over the interests of blacks, and the interests of men continue to be promoted over the interests of women. The black woman's unique experience as a member of two distinctly disadvantaged groups (black and female) is thereby erased.

It is most distressing to read the written work of black women writers, like the author of the *Black Man's Guide*, who are so anxious to gain benefits from white America's patriarchal class system that they are willing to deny or distort their own unique experience as black women in America. Perhaps I should not be surprised in light of the history of the black African countries in which black African citizens sold other black African citizens to the vicious white slave traders. In spite of the many well-deserved criticisms that fall upon the head of the white male, the white male has not been the only villain in the scourge of slavery that continues to haunt us today.

How often we hear that the Fifteenth Amendment gave blacks the right to vote when in reality, this amendment gave nothing to black women except perhaps another master. In explaining the history of discrimination against women in America, historians and academicians alike note the general solicitude society has accorded women because of concerns that women needed special protection, when in reality, black women have worked in the fields doing the same work that black men have done, even after the "emancipation," and have never been accorded any special solicitude by American society.

Our obsession with "the white man's obsession" with destroying the black male's masculinity causes us to completely overlook the fact that though stripped of his patriarchal status the black male was never forced to assume a feminine role or perform so-called feminine tasks that cut against the grain of society's defined masculine gender role. The black female, however, was forced to perform tasks distinctly defined as masculine, such as plowing fields, picking cotton and laying track for the railroads. Thus it may be more accurate to say that the institution of slavery attempted to strip the black female of the accepted societal gender role rather than the black male. Society clearly was not concerned that black women needed special protection.

Almost as perversely, we hear arguments that American "women" have not achieved economic parity with men because "women" have not been in the marketplace as long as men, when in reality, the black woman has been in the marketplace since she was brought to America on the first slave ship, raped and brutalized en route. One can only conclude that black women are not women or blacks, as statements about women and blacks routinely exclude the black woman's experience.

In commenting on the plight of black women in America, an early black suffragist aptly noted, "We are the slaves of slaves; we are exploited more ruthlessly than men."[2] Few have appreciated the irony of her words. Little scholarly attention has been given to the oppression of black women because of the sexist assumption that the experiences of men are more important than those of women and that what matters most among the experiences of men is their ability to assert themselves patriarchally. *The Black Man's Guide* clearly promotes this chauvinistic, misogynous mind set. It would be difficult indeed to believe that a book so misogynous and chauvinistic could have been written by a black woman and so well received by black America, if not for Phyllis

Schafly's warm reception in the hearts and minds of white America. If white America can believe that a woman can save her marriage by greeting her husband at the door dressed in Saran wrap, I suppose I should not be surprised that black America too would readily embrace drivel where the role of black women is concerned. Ours truly is an androcentric society, whatever the color of the man.

Unfortunately, many black men, as well as most whites, seem will-fully, blissfully ignorant of the double bind of black women in America. On the one hand, the black woman who is not dependent and submis-sive is viewed as a castrating bitch. On the other hand, the black woman who is submissive and dependent upon a black man finds sur-vival very difficult in a society in which: (1) large numbers of black males have criminal records or are illiterate and are thereby effectively eliminated from the job market even if all discrimination were to end tomorrow; (2) large numbers of black men prefer white women over black women; (3) even those black men who express a preference for black women generally do not marry black women of a complexion darker than themselves; (4) even if a black man marries a black woman he will likely have difficulty supporting her and a family.

Perhaps this willful ignorance stems in part from the inaccurate por-trayal of the black woman's experience in this country. The experience of the black woman is different from that of the black man or the white woman. Black women are not black men, nor are they white women. Society's convenient lumping of black women into either category does not change this reality, at least for the black women affected.

Black women have never ascended the pedestal. Furthermore, in addition to being oppressed by white men and white women, black women have been oppressed by black men, physically, mentally, and spiritually. The only group in America with a lower status than black females is children. In the oppression of women, black men have been no more noble than white men. Both have used their power, be it the power of the dollar or the power of the fist, and resources to keep women "in their place." In the oppression of women, all men are broth-ers—black, white, yellow, brown, and red alike. No doubt if there are women on Mars, they too are oppressed by their male counterparts. The extent to which black women are oppressed is ignored by the media, both black and white.

Neither my childhood experience nor my upbringing is consistent with the images presented in the mass media, black or white. The white media would have us believe that all blacks were born and raised in big city ghettos and that the "black problem" is confined to the ghetto. Therefore as long as there is no ghetto in the immediate vicinity, racism is not a problem. The black media would have us believe that black

7

women have already been "liberated" because black males are somehow more noble than their white male counterparts in that black men are immune to sexism and the concomitant oppression of women. Both propositions are patently false.

Like millions of other black women raised in the South, I did not grow up on welfare or in the midst of a sprawling urban ghetto in which families were stacked on top of each other like sardines. Most families in the black communities that I knew, even those who were dirt poor, lived in houses, whether owned or rented, not apartment buildings. Often the houses were old, run down and in desperate need of repairs, but even when overt racism was rampant and Jim Crow was the order of the day, there were always a few "Sugar Hills" for those blacks who managed to overcome the living hell of being black in America.

The shotgun houses were the most decrepit houses of all. They were usually no more than a few rooms in size. The interior of every room in the house was visible from the front door. One could stand looking in the front door with a telescopic view of every room in the house, and at the same time look directly out the back door, much like looking down the barrel of a shotgun. (Hence the name.) The standing joke was that one shotgun blast would kill every nigger in the house. The few housing projects that did exist were never more than two stories tall and not so massive as to be cities within themselves.

Unlike the black female child presented in the *Black Man's Guide*, I had little opportunity to learn how to "scam" on the black man from my mother. Even if she had learned how to "scam" from her no-nonsense mother, my mother, who had eight children and a full-time job, was simply too busy with the mundane tasks that are associated with raising eight children to teach me the fine art of "scamming". She was so busy cooking, cleaning, washing, ironing, sweeping, etc., that we had little time to learn much about her, except that she was a virtual slave in her own home. Like the corporate mother so condemned today, my mother was always busy, not with the business of the firm, but with the business of raising an army of children.

Unlike the child in the *Black Man's Guide*, I was not privileged to conversations between my mother and her friends or relatives pertaining to my father. My mother had few friends. In the eighteen years that I lived in my parents' home, I can count on one hand the number of times that friends came to the house to socialize with my mother. She did not have time to socialize. My mother had little time to confide in her children or anyone else about my father. The only way to claim her undivided attention was to get sick. Otherwise, my mother spent her days running from chore to chore.

8

One thing I did learn from watching my mother was that I did not want to meet a similar fate. I have never been able to understand the logic of working every day yet being so poor that the services of a dentist were a luxury the family could not afford, or spending hours cooking and cleaning at night, yet facing the same dirty dishes and floors the next day. Even as a child I sensed that life was somehow unfair to women. We were trapped within the fences that surrounded our homes, whether those fences were real or imaginary.

Sometimes I wished I were a boy so that I could escape the fence. As a boy, I would not have to endure the agony of having my hair straightened with a hot comb to make myself presentable and could help my father cut the grass on Saturdays instead of the daily grind of sweeping, dusting, and washing dishes. On the occasions when my father would cut grass for white people in neighborhoods I had never seen, I would beg to go. Sometimes daddy would take my brothers, but never me. My "place" was in the house where the world was safe from my inquisitive and prying eyes. Adventures were not for black girls unless they read them in books. And so I retreated to books and worlds in which I was free.

I have always suspected that the disparate treatment in childhood is part of the reason girls generally make better students than boys. Boys are allowed to learn from experience, girls are forced to learn from books.

I grew to hate my "place," but whenever my father scolded me to "Go back into the house with your mother before you turn out to be a tomboy," I would bow my head and go back inside. To me, the house always seemed dark compared with the brilliant outdoors. I swore to myself that when I grew up, if ever I had a daughter, I would not be so cruel to her. I have never had a daughter, but if I did I would be happy for her to cut grass and work on cars. I would not want to limit her childhood experiences the way mine were limited.

On my first trip home from college, I saw how limited my world truly was. For the first time I saw my world through the eyes of an outsider and realized how precarious a position I occupied relative to the world around me. For the first time, I noticed that every tooth in my mother's head was decayed. But, she always smiled broadly like the proud bird she was. She never spent a dime on herself for fear that one of her children would lack something. She always ate the piece of chicken that no one wanted or the slice of toast that got burned. She used to tell us that the end slice of bread was the best slice in the loaf, and contented herself with that.

When my father was so sick with ulcers that he had to have surgery and could not work for a long time, my mother's wedding ring disappeared. I believe she pawned it and was never able to retrieve it. My father, who never had more than two pair of shoes at a time in his life, used to tease my mother about her run over shoes. I made up my mind early on that I would not live as a slave in my own home or wear run-over shoes, even if it meant not having a man. To date, I have no man but I do own about forty pairs of shoes.

My first trip home from college was also memorable in that my ne'er-do-well uncle murdered both my favorite aunt (his wife) and my grandmother. I looked so much like my aunt that on occasion I was mistaken for the daughter that she never had. My aunt was always flattered. She was never as flattered as I was because I knew I could not be as beautiful as she. Even her laughter was beautiful, sounding of delicate bell chimes ringing in a gentle breeze. After twenty years of enduring hard times and my uncle's drinking, gambling, and other women, my desperate aunt had decided to leave her husband. She was quite sick and my grandparents helped her find an apartment so that she could heal in peace. I had never seen her look so poorly.

My grandmother was taking my aunt to the doctor when my uncle drove by in his hopped-up car and shotgunned both of them to death in full view of my cousin (their son), who was opening the car door for his mother. So much of my grandmother's head was blown away that her casket could not be opened at the funeral. My grown cousin, who at 6 foot 4 inches was the most gentle giant I have ever known, could only cry, "Daddy, why?" as he stood soaked in blood and fragmented body tissue and watched his mother bleed to death on the sidewalk. Mercifully, our grandmother had died instantaneously. Part of my grandfather died with her.

I was nineteen years old and for the first time in my life I sensed how estranged we really were from white America. There was no public outcry at the deaths of my grandmother and aunt. Their deaths were business as usual—nigger business, that is. My uncle pleaded temporary insanity and was back on the streets in a few years. No one was outraged that he had brutally murdered 2 loving and beautiful people, one of whom was a college professor, like her father before her—my grief-stricken grandfather. No one was enraged that my uncle had perhaps permanently damaged his own son's mind.

Brutality was not new to me. As a child, I had been left with a baby sitter who frequently beat my older sister and me, and locked us in the closet the moment my parents were out of sight. She threatened to cut our tongues and hearts out if we told. Because Mildred was smart enough not to leave any scars, our parents never believed our stories about her until the day that my mother came home early and caught Mildred beating my sister while I was locked up in an outside shed. I was so afraid of Mildred that my own mother could not get me to come out of the shed without Mildred's permission until I was sure that Mildred had gone home and would not be there to punish me should she catch me disobeying her order to stay inside the shed. I remember peeping through a knot-hole under a bench in the shed until I saw Mildred get into a car and leave. Only then did I feel that it was safe to leave the shed.

Four years ago when I asked my mother whatever happened to Mildred, she was surprised that I still remembered the name. I can picture Mildred wearing my mother's white chenille robe with blue flowers and waving the scissors menacingly at us as she was fond to do thirty-seven years ago, even though I was only three years old at the time. Mildred is currently in jail for knifing a man to death.

Brutality against adult women was not new to me either. Though my father never beat my mother, I had two other uncles (one of whom was eventually shot in the head by an unknown robber) who were known womanizers and on occasion beat their wives fiercely. For all I know they could have beat their girlfriends, too. I never inquired. However, I had never dreamed that the violence between a man and his wife could turn into murder.

If, as the *Black Man's Guide* suggests, men are to be allowed to "discipline" women who displease them, at what point does "discipline" degenerate into permanent maiming or murder? What assurance does any woman have that she will not be killed? At nineteen, as I sat at my dead aunt's wake listening to my giant cousin cry and watching the familiar image of myself lying in my dead aunt's casket, for the first time in my life, I sensed how precarious my position in life as a black woman truly was—damned because I was black, damned because I was a woman. I have been running scared ever since.

Even now, twenty years and six states later, I sometimes wake up in the middle of the night sweating and panic-stricken, not grieving for my long dead grandmother and aunt, but fearful that there is no safe harbor for women like me, castoffs in a white society. The nightmare is always the same. Something huge and hideous that sucks the very oxygen from the air is chasing me. No matter how fast I run, which way I turn or where I try to hide, the horror is always one step behind, breathing down my neck. The stale hot air is oppressive. Sometimes when I lie half asleep and half awake, I hear it breathing and growing stronger outside my bedroom door, as if it were feeding on my fear and could only sustain itself by keeping me in a state of constant terror.

I never look behind me in these dreams because I know that always I am a hair's breadth from disaster. Only when I wrench myself completely from slumber and sit bolt upright gasping for breath does the horror slink away. If I go back to sleep, the dream starts all over again. It is a cruel game. I fight to stay awake, until overcome by exhaustion, I succumb to sleep. There is no one to save me, except daybreak, so I continue to run looking for the safe harbor that is never there, until the sun rises and chases away the fate that waits to ensnare me.

The media do not tell the story of black women like me. There is no special solicitude or protection for us. Unlike the kind and gentle white woman, we are viewed as evil and quarrelsome or competitive. We are called Sapphires. If we are independent enough to support our families without men, we are told we should sit down or change our behavior and wait for a man to take care of us. If we are so dependent that when there is no man we resort to welfare, we are scorned as welfare queens. We are damned if we do, and damned if we do not.

Literature like the *Black Man's Guide* and the *Moynihan Report* tell the world that black women have caused the downfall of the black race by competing with black males in the marketplace. The *Black Man's Guide* tells us that if only the black man could get us in line, he could rise to his rightful place as master of the universe. While the white men responsible for the *Moynihan Report* did not go so far as to acknowledge that the black man should be master of the universe, the report did suggest that the black man could regain his self-esteem through domination of the black woman. According to the *Moynihan Report*:

> Ours is a society which presumes male leadership in
> private and public affairs. The arrangements of society
> facilitate such leadership and reward it. A subculture,
> such as that of the Negro American, in which this is not
> the pattern, is placed at a distinct disadvantage.[3]

To those who do not understand the life experiences of black women like me, perhaps we appear hard, cold or aloof. We are, however, the products of our environment, an environment that is often very cruel. Because of my experiences as a black child, I am ever mindful of the pitfalls that await me as a black woman. The dark shadow that haunts my sleep is a constant reminder.

Those men who follow the advice in the *Black Man's Guide* that black women want and need discipline should be forewarned that many sisters will leave without so much as a goodbye the first time a hand is raised to us. Others will strike back lest they meet the fate of so many black women who failed to defend themselves. Black women have seen enough of violence and tragedy.

Also, whether or not it pleases a male companion, many sisters have no interest in casual or unprotected sex and the associated risk of an unwanted pregnancy. We have seen enough of the poverty and despair of abandoned black women with hungry children to feed, children who cannot understand why Santa is so stingy or why the tooth-fairy never comes. We have no interest in trusting in the Lord to provide for us or to take care of problems that we may either take care of ourselves, or avoid altogether by setting goals, planning, and using some common sense. We have seen enough of the unanswered prayers of grey-headed old women and desperate young ones. We can no longer wait for miracles that, like the revolution, never come to set us free. We have no interest in letting someone else make major decisions in our lives simply because he happens to have a penis or cloak himself with the authority of a god that has done little for him either—that is, unless he happens to be the one taking up the collection plate.

For many black women who have watched their sisters suffer needlessly at the hand of some black male, the measure of a man is his deeds, not his penis, his position, his ego, his authority or his words. Reality sounds much louder than speech or dreams for black women. Dreams have their place but reality for black women in America is harsh.

Reality for black women in America usually means work, generally unfulfilling and mundane work in a lower echelon capacity with a correspondingly low wage. The *Black Man's Guide* and frequently the black community's insistent focus on the well-to-do black woman of corporate America when discussing the problems of the black family is ludicrous. Considering that only 11% of blacks have college degrees,[4] and that an even smaller number of these graduates are able to penetrate the invisible corporate barriers and glass ceilings, these well-heeled sisters probably represent less than 2 to 3 percent of black American women. And yet when focusing on the problems in the black community and the so-called emasculation of the black male by the competitive black female, we choose to focus on the overachieving, superstar sisters to escape the harsh reality of the abhorrent condition of life for many of the other 98 percent of black women in America.

No one wants to acknowledge the reality of the generations of black women who have dealt with daily threats of physical and sexual abuse in the marketplace, for the privilege of cleaning public toilets, scrubbing floors, and taking care of other women's children (while their own languished at home) just so that their families would have food, clothing and shelter. Until World War II, black women were relegated to the fringes of the economy as agricultural sharecroppers and domestic servants. Many of the service jobs black women performed put them in daily contact with racist whites, both male and female, who abused, humiliated and tormented them. These women could well have felt the intensity of de-humanization much more intensely than the black males who spent their days on the street corners, free of the menial jobs that

13

would have subjected them to the personal indignities inflicted by racist whites. Typical of the bind in which black women find themselves, the black mother who considers herself "too good" to resort to menial labor to provide for her children is considered "uppity," while the black mother who resorts to welfare is considered "lazy." Black women cannot win for losing.

If we turn our focus to the black agricultural and service workers and housemaids, it is difficult indeed to perpetuate the myth that the white man has always been willing to help the black woman and that the white woman has sympathetically welcomed the black woman as a sister or ally. The white man has helped himself to the black woman's body and her labor, but has done little for her, while for the most part the white woman has stood idly by, afraid to threaten her own precarious perch. Even if whites had been willing to hire black males as nursemaids, cleaning women and washwomen, black men would no doubt have refused these jobs as an assault on male dignity, as would many today.

In the period around World War II when black women began to claim industrial jobs, hostility between black and white female workers was the norm. To prevent white employers from hiring black women workers, white females frequently threatened to quit. Often separate work rooms, washrooms, and showers were installed so that white women would not have to work or wash next to black women. And yet these struggling black female workers are portrayed primarily as enjoying advantages the black man was denied. Working for low wages at jobs reserved for those ranked lowest in the American caste system does not increase one's self esteem. Only a profound commitment to the greater good of one's family can make these jobs even bearable.

To suggest that we should be ashamed of the legacy of the black women who braved the hostile marketplace or that these women should have remained at home so that black men, like white men, could have the opportunity to pick and choose among the women they want in the marriage meat market, while those women not selected face poverty and neglect, is simple-minded and idiotic. Single women have as much stake in America as married ones. Instead of aping the white man and mindlessly assisting him in institutionalizing his patriarchal class system wherever he sets foot, black men and women would do well to try to implement a more humane institution.

Reasoning that the black man should be lord and master of the black woman because the white man is lord and master of the white woman is about as logical as suggesting that we enslave the Vietnamese, since they appear to be hardy workers able to endure great hardship, and make them the new niggers of America so that the black race can rise like the white race did, on the backs of another race. I would want no part of such insanity because I know what it is like to be despised simply because of my appearance.

I am proud of the generations of black women who did what they had to do to survive. To those who submitted to whatever indignity they had to in order to insure my survival, I say thank you. What choice did these women have? The black man was equally as shackled as the black woman and neither Jesus nor Big Brother was around to save either. Nothing or no one could save these desperate black women except their own blood, sweat and tears. Past generations of black Americans would not have survived if these caring black women had refused to accept and perform work that was beneath the dignity of the woman's so-called place in the home. A woman's place is wherever she needs to be to ensure her survival.

The black women today who choose to and are able to survive solely as homemakers are fortunate indeed. However, there is no point in the rest of us deceiving ourselves. We have no choice but to educate ourselves and fight for a living in the current labor market, not the idealized one where all God's children are free and have shoes. There are no black knights in shining armor for us and for large numbers of us there never will be. Life is harsh for black women who cannot support themselves.

The old black women we see every day with all their belongings in shopping bags are a harsh reminder. All of these women are not crazy and many have raised families. And yet these women spend their days in public libraries and their nights on public buses (if the bus driver is kind). This cruel fate awaits many of our beautiful young girls.

In reality, black women must work not only for their own survival but for the survival of their children. No matter how practical, or clever or self-denying a woman is, if her husband makes little more than minimum wage, the woman has little choice but to work or to watch her husband work himself into an early grave trying to be the sole provider for his family, an all too often impossible task. Black women who aspire to be housewives may have an admirable goal, but they are bucking tough odds and should be prepared to pick themselves up from the hard blows that are likely to come.

Despite the fact that the materialistic black woman is made to blame for the impossibility of making ends meet with the meager paychecks of so many black men, in many instances it is the number of offspring produced that stretch the husband's check past sufficiency, not the wife's extravagant spending. After any pie is cut into so many thin slices, the slices become crumbs. The black men who are so quick to harangue the black woman for her extravagant spending should instead consider assuming more responsibility for birth control and family planning, or be willing to accept a limited lifestyle without blaming the wife. Likewise, the women who choose to remain at home with the children may as well accept the reality of a limited lifestyle without blaming the husband for the fact that it is difficult indeed for a black man in America to make as much money as a white man.

Had my mother not worked outside the home, our family of ten simply could not have survived on my father's salary, in spite of his good intentions and college education. In spite of my parent's indefatigable faith, Jesus never made the bread or fish or anything else at our house multiply, except perhaps the babies. My father used to set traps in a nearby creek to catch the fish we ate. The rest were bought at the grocery store, sometimes on credit.

Our yard was filled with fruit trees instead of ornamental shrubbery. Many poor southern men like my father who grew up on dirt farms rather than on asphalt basketball courts like their also poor big city northern counterparts, were good hunters and horticulturists. Oftentimes our table was filled with wild game. A man with practical skills can almost always feed his family without resorting to crime. A man whose skills are limited to those that allow him to survive on the corner will often have difficulty feeding even himself. He will have little choice but to resort to crime since little in life is free and few people are going to give him anything.

That black men do not make as much money as white men is not a criticism of black men. It is simply an unpleasant statement of fact. That the average black woman does not make as much money as the average white women or the average black man is equally as unpleasant. However, this is the reality the black woman must face, especially if she plans to exercise her procreative capacity and faces extended periods where she either cannot or chooses not to work. Black women who ignore this reality do so at their potential peril.

It is incredible that today's black woman who seeks to curb the size of her family is condemned as not raising soldiers for the revolution. Few women, black or white and however talented, are capable of effectively administering to the physical, psychological and emotional needs of more than a handful of children, whether employed or unemployed. Wealthy women do not hire housekeepers solely because they are lazy. They hire housekeepers in part because maintaining a home is not only hard work but often unrewarding.

Magically, the same grubby handprints appear on the refrigerator door each day at sunrise, as does the ring in the bathtub, the ring in the toilet, and the ring around the collar. The demands of children (not to mention a husband) are simply too great for anyone to pretend that housework is easy. Additionally, all the hard work in the world does not guarantee that one's children will not decide that they had rather be bums or dopers. Children do have minds of their own that even their parents cannot always control.

The good earth mother who can magically solve all problems with her soothing touch, no matter how overburdened she is, is a childhood myth that was not debunked by the *Black Man's Guide*, perhaps deliberately so, since the author short-sightedly suggested that the soothing touch of a worshipful black woman is the answer to the problems facing the black man. If racism were to go away tomorrow, black men without the skills valued in the labor market, or with criminal records still would not find employment, no matter how much or how many black women truly loved and respected them. The black men who are well-equipped for the labor market can and will succeed *with or without* the black woman once whites stop throwing stumbling blocks in the path. Likewise, black women who are well-equipped will succeed with or without the black man once artificial barriers are removed from their paths. Those who think that their black skin makes them indispensable to their black mates surely have not opened their eyes lately.

The world is so overpopulated that none of us is indispensable or irreplaceable in spite of our delusions of grandeur. It makes no more sense to say that blacks are the superior race than to say that whites are the superior race. Men are just men and women are just women. When will the "we're number one" insanity end? There has never been peace on earth because of man's infernal desire to be number one and dominate the world. There is no "eternal peace"[5] in Africa either. Black African males and their system of government have proved themselves to be just as oppressive and corrupt as white males and their system of government.

Those blacks who fancy black men "the greatest form of life on the planet"[6] and "rulers of the universe and everything in it"[7] have surely forgotten the last world war and the dangers of racial superiority theory. Before the end of the war, millions died in the wake of death and destruction created by the last wave of "the greatest form of life on the planet," the Aryan supremacists. Their legacy lives on in the skinheads of America, who claim the God-given right to rule those who are not members of the master race.

The destructive legacy of white supremacy, has changed the gene pool of the black race in America and has resulted in a race of people so stigmatized by color alone that blacks of different shades have been known to discriminate against each other on the basis of color. "If you're light, you're alright; if you're brown, stick around; but if you're black, get back" is an old chant that has been used to annoy many darker-skinned

17

blacks. Green eyes, yellow skin, and stringy hair have been valuable assets to many blacks not only in the white community but in the black community as well.

Those blacks who think that the world cannot survive without them have but to observe the now predominantly immigrant hotel service industry that was once predominantly black to see how quickly they can be replaced. Gone are the grand old gray-haired black men who used to stand outside of the palatial hotels where most poor black people never ventured, in their magnificent uniforms with shiny brass buttons and heavy epaulets. These regal-looking black men always gave a nod or a wink to the awe-struck black children who walked past and sometimes called out, "Good day sir," to our dads as if there really were a black brotherhood.

Those whites who used to complain about the poor English of working class blacks are suddenly content to deal with workers who speak no English at all. Those blacks who view the loss of the hotel service industry as a sign of progress are no doubt blacks who are not among the ranks of the unfortunate blacks who could find work only in that service industry.

Sadly, before most of our bodies are cold or in the ground, someone will be waiting to step into the place left empty by our deaths. The sun will rise and set tomorrow with or without the black man or black woman. Those who do not survive are quickly forgotten. History has been able to repeat itself for thousands of years precisely because we forget so quickly. The human memory is short and fickle.

Kicking the dog or blaming the black woman for the problems of the black race is senseless when it is the racist marketplace that creates the problem. Kicking the dog may vent frustrations, but it will not change the marketplace. Likewise, changing the black woman will not change the marketplace or the obstacles black men face. There is no magic or miracle cure ahead for blacks, only grinding hard work whether it is fair or not, and whether we like it or not.

The thousands of black males in our communities who graduate (or fail to graduate) illiterate or semi-literate but who nonetheless have families will never find jobs to support those families in the present marketplace. It is tragic comedy to suggest that black women are taking jobs away from the large numbers of black men whom no employer will ever hire because of their illiteracy and criminal records. Those who dropout hammer the nails in their own coffins since one's future in America is generally determined in large part by one's high school transcript. On the basis of a high school transcript alone, doors may be opened or permanently closed. It is a pity that so many youths think that life starts when they "grow up." In reality it starts in the 10th grade. Those who stumble there will spend the remainder of their lives trying to catch up.

There is no point in deceiving these youths into thinking that they have a chance in life as dropouts, so that they can "feel good about themselves." Feeling good about oneself will not get one a job, but a diploma might. In this country, "no diploma" virtually guarantees "no life." It is virtually impossible to "get a life" without first getting at least a high school diploma. Those who fail to get a high school diploma need not complain about racism because they are not even in the game. For all practical purposes they are dead, but have yet to be buried. As they rot and decay, the neighborhoods around them decay. When the stench becomes too great, the walking dead will be buried in jail cells, mental institutions or the military if they are lucky. Drug overdoses and drive-by shootings save the government the expense of their burial.

As for the 11 percent of blacks who do graduate from college and go on to become professionals, our focus is skewed. It is the other 89 percent of the black population surviving at the margins that we should be worried about. However, even among the so-called elite group, black males make more than black females. If one chooses to compare apples and oranges, and compares a black female doctor or lawyer with a black male blue-collar worker (just because one assumes that a man should make more money than a woman), then of course the black female enjoys some advantages. However the comparison is irrational because the two workers operate in different realms with different rules and qualifications, all of which are set by whites. The rational comparison would be one between a black female professional and a black male professional.

If a black female professional is compared with the black male professional in her peer group, she enjoys no advantage. She usually makes less money than her professional black male counterpart, and her children and husband make demands of her when she goes home just as every woman's children and husband make demands. Mom is always expected to sacrifice her needs to everyone else's.

In those areas where there appear to be more female professionals, it would be odd if such were not the case in light of: (1) the large numbers of black males who are permanently disqualified from the elite professions because of their criminal records; (2) the fact that there are naturally more black females in the population than black males, and past wars in addition to black-on-black homicide have increased the disparity between the numbers of black females and black males in the population; (3) the fact that a disproportionately high number of black males drop out of the educational pool at the threshold levels (high school and below) and thus the number of black males in the educational pool at the upper level is permanently disproportionately diminished, even if racism were non-existent; (4) the fact that the illiteracy rate for black males is higher than the illiteracy rate for black females. The assumption that there should be more black male professionals than black female professionals has no rational basis, unless one ignores reality and blindly assumes that the black community should mirror the white community, in spite of the fact that it never has. The time spent blaming black females for black males' poor performance in the marketplace would be better spent correcting the social ills that cause that poor performance.

Although all my life I have heard how easy black women have it being a "double minority," I have never been fortunate enough to land one of the jobs where such was the case. The black female professionals that I know have resigned themselves to the reality that in the eyes of their white colleagues they are not equal and never will be. Therefore black female professionals have little choice but to work harder than their colleagues, often for less money. In spite of what the *Black Man's Guide* suggests, these women do not hang around the office until all hours of the night because they enjoy the company of white people.

It is ironic that in spite of the fact that black women are supposed to be more educated than black men, the average black male worker makes more than the average black female worker (or the average white female worker) at all levels. This differential is not due to the black man's (or any man's) clever ability to beat the system. Instead, it is due to precisely the way the system is designed to operate. The differential is the result of the discrimination on the basis of sex with which every woman must contend, most particularly, the black woman. All men enjoy certain advantages because of their sex, including the black man. Though he rails against the discrimination against him on the basis of his race, the black man is often silent about the discrimination against the black woman because of her sex, and often participates in this discrimination, just as oppressively as the white male.

As usual, the black woman is supposed to sacrifice her economic interests for the good of the black race, in spite of the fact that she is often the only source of support for her family. Sapphire is supposed to keep her mouth shut about sex discrimination (otherwise she is accused of being divisive) until the black man gets what the white man owes him, and then the black man will take care of the black woman, or so the story goes. Unfortunately, all too often, by the time the black man begins to collect what is due him, he has forgotten all about Sapphire and her problems. So Sapphire must continue to fend for herself and her children. Her undying love is no longer needed and the little soldiers she has been encouraged to bring into the world for the revolution are then viewed as a pain in the ass.

Even if the black man forever wanted the black woman's undying love, the black woman's offering of this love and submission would not automatically create a place in the job market for the black man. Romantic myth should not be confused with economic reality. The love between a man and a woman cannot overcome racism in the marketplace. Additionally, even those employers who are willing to ignore skin color or who are forced to disregard skin color are not willing to ignore a lack of the required credentials. We can debate the reasonableness of the credential requirements forever, but it will not change the employers' requirements for credentials. Debate will not change the fact that in spite of the shortsightedness of their reasoning, most employers are not interested in what a potential employee can do, but instead, what that employee has done. No track record equals no job. And yet we continue to talk about changing the black woman instead of changing the marketplace or black men.

Changing the black woman or getting love from the black woman will not change the capitalist system within which we live and from which we must extract resources to survive in America, or improve the black man's position in the capitalist market. Those who think the current distribution of goods and services unfair, might better expend their energy trying to change the system, rather than change the black woman. It is the system that is unfair, not the so-called quarrelsome black woman alluded to in the *Black Man's Guide*. Sapphire is only a scapegoat for those who choose to place the responsibility for their poor performance on the black woman.

Those who focus on changing the black woman, like the *Black Man's Guide*, but who choose to ignore the current plight of black women by suggesting that black women learn to live in this world but not of this world would make good disciples in the ranks of the Nancy Reagan "Just say no!" campaign. Both views are equally unrealistic. Outside influences commence working on a child before he or she leaves the mother's womb in a delivery room. Many babies have been shot or stabbed while still in their mothers' womb. Addicted babies are born every day without knowing anything about the drug they are hooked on or that they are hooked or even what a drug is. Thus outside influences pierce even the mother's womb. The television brings outside influences into the home in living technicolor, as does the neighbor's kid when he or she comes over to play. Living in a vacuum is a temporary solution that allows escape from reality only for a while. Outside influences affect every child in America.

The message these influences feed to black females from the day they come into the world is that they are the lowest of the low. They are worse than niggers! They are nigger women, nigger bitches and "hoes"

21

in the street vernacular. Whether a black woman's hair is permed, naturally straight, curly or kinky; whether she wears too much make-up or no make-up at all; whether she is obsequious and fawning or overly aggressive; whether she is young or old, fat or thin; whether she has a Ph.D. or is illiterate, she is still called nigger bitch and will encounter a rocky road not only in the outside world but often in her own family.

If she dares to complain, she becomes worse than a nigger bitch. She becomes the evil Sapphire, the contentious sister from hell whose mission in life is to make life miserable for the black man. The black comedians know her well and love to tell us about her. They have carried on a love affair with Sapphire for years, though generally these comedians prefer to marry white women. Sapphire has helped make dick-grabbing comedians like Eddie Murphy famous, while her friends, lovers and those sworn to protect her sat by and laughed. "You've gotta admit the nigger is funny!" they offer as consolation.

No one bothers to ask why black comedians do not trash white women. No doubt these same comedians would not be considered "funny" anymore if they turned their venom on white women. In fact, they would probably die old and broke (i.e., if some irate white man did not kill them while they were young) instead of enjoying their current fame and wealth in our system of peculiar double standards. This is cruel reality for many black women in America.

When it comes to raising children, reality for all women is that, few men, black or white, are even interested in administering to the needs of more than a handful of children. The family law courts across America are filled with the tragic stories of children whose fathers have lost interest in administering to the needs of their children when the burden became too great. These stories cut across all race and class lines.

In spite of what the patriarchs profess, the desire to provide is not an innate male instinct. Surveys of groups of women from all races and classes who are stymied in collecting child support payments from ex-husbands provide ample evidence of men's reluctance to assume the provider role. When the stress factor becomes too great for most males, they simply move on, doctor, lawyer, and itinerant painter alike. At that point, the fact that their wives and lovers are submissive and dependent upon them then becomes a major hindrance and annoyance. At this point the submissive and dependent housewife is told she should now "get a job," whether she has 3 or 4 toddlers at home or is 55 years old and has been out of the job market for 35 years. The elderly white woman may be granted rehabilitative alimony with which to retrain herself, but the mystery remains as to what she should train herself to do (law school or medical school perhaps) or who will hire this elderly woman with no track record. It is funny how things change when men become inconvenienced.

When I see women with large numbers of children, I shudder because I know they will experience great difficulty splitting themselves into the dozen or so different entities required to fulfill all the unrealistic roles our I-can-bring-home-the-bacon-fry-it-up-in-a-pan-and-then-spend-all-night-making-love-to-my-man society places on women. Being a housewife is demanding, whether the woman has an outside job or not. The woman who has outside help come in 2 or 3 times a week to do her dirty work cannot begin to be compared to the woman who must do all her own housework. And yet both are expected to greet hubby at the door with a glass of champagne (or beer) and a smile.

Another popular myth touted by the *Black Man's Guide*, is that mothers who stay at home and produce large numbers of offspring are sustaining the black nation by producing soldiers for the revolution. But in reality, many of these mothers do not get the help they need and wind up juggling more tasks than they should have to handle at great costs to themselves and their children. Mothers have needs just like their children and husbands. Needs that are ignored fester and grow wherever they can find root. Eventually the pressure will find a way to release itself. Producing large numbers of offspring may be an admirable goal; indeed it is challenging and requires much devotion. However, those who choose this option should acknowledge that they are merely doing what they want to do, rather than try to lay a guilt trip on the women whose families cannot afford for them to stay home and raise soldiers, or who make other choices. Women are not necessarily born to breed.

As for the teenage mothers who are children themselves, only a fool could suggest that they are birthing the black nation of tomorrow, as does the *Black Man's Guide*.[8] If anything, these girls are helping to destroy the black nation of tomorrow with their legacy of unwanted, misguided, ill-prepared and all too often mentally and physically defective and subsequently abandoned babies. Those who condone the births of these troubled children should go to the hospital wards where these babies languish and take them home. Perhaps this way the babies will have half a chance at life instead of no chance at all.

How many citizens in the black community will have their lives ruined by the future marauding of the babies these young girls are dumping on the street corners of America? Once these babies outgrow their playpens and can no longer be held captive in the public schools, the very adults who cooed and ahhhed at them when they were helpless infants will now consider these grown infants dangerous. Once these children are labelled disturbed and menaces to society, L.A.P.D.'s finest will be unleashed to do a Rodney King number on the now unsympathetic babes who have completed the transition from Dr. Jekyll to Mr. Hyde.

How will the crack babies, whose attention span is limited to 5 minutes or less, ever develop into productive citizens capable of maintaining families? In the future, are these neglected children to be punished for neglecting their families when all they have ever known is neglect? Who will take care of the babies of the children having children, or of the babies of the babies of the children having children? How long before the carnage of our own black youth surpasses the carnage of slavery? At least as slaves blacks had some economic worth to society, if nothing else. To the gang-bangers, hop-heads and dope dealers that set up shop in the black communities where large numbers of disadvantaged children live, a black human life has no worth whatsoever.

The use of birth control and family planning could make life much easier not only for women, but their families as well. There simply is not always room for one more. No child should be an accident. This is not to say that women should be charged with total responsibility for birth control and family planning. However, harsh reality has shown that when the family unit breaks down, it is usually the woman who falls heir to the responsibility of the children.

After divorce and subsequent inability to collect child support from my ex-husband, I reproached him for his seeming lack of concern for his child's well being. To my surprise, he commented that he was not concerned about our child's welfare because he knew that I would take care of the child, whatever it took.

At present, my son has not seen his father in ten years. Nor did he have any idea of his father's whereabouts until last spring. There was never a phone call, a letter, or even a birthday card until last spring when a letter written from a jail cell arrived at my parent's home, addressed to my son. Even though he barely remembered his father, he was heartbroken to learn that his father had chosen to live the criminal life. Most distressing, we learned from another source that one of the charges against his father involved the battery and confinement of his live-in lover's young daughter. It was only after his father had burned every bridge in life that he ever had and was left with nowhere else to turn that he turned to his son, expecting that his son would be concerned enough to write him while he was in jail.

My ex-husband, who is a college graduate from a big-ten university and former honorable mention All-American football player, has been out of jail for a while now and has yet to send his son a penny. He knows that I am juggling work, law school and my law school tuition, and tuition for our son's private school. At 15, my son is 6 foot 2 inches tall, weighs 200 pounds, wears a size 13 D shoe and plays two musical instruments. His upkeep is very expensive. This summer, he found his first job. He is working at a movie theater in Westwood for a little over minimum wage. Even so, he will make more in one summer than he has gotten from his father in 12 years. The agreed upon child support was only $35/week.

When I mentioned to his father recently that I could use the years of back child support, he informed me that he plans to get his life together by going back to school soon and therefore remains short of funds. I never asked where he thought the funds came from for me to feed and clothe his son while at the same time finish my undergraduate degree and go to law school. I am sure the thought never entered his head. Like so many men, he has been trained to think of the world only in terms of his own needs. Everything else is secondary.

In the twelve years since my divorce, I have observed that my ex-husband's comment that I would provide for the child holds true for women across all walks of life, from the divorced law school dean to the divorced or never-married mothers on the law school janitorial staff. In this single aspect, we are all sisters. Women across class and race lines will generally provide for their offspring at great inconvenience to themselves. The tragedy is that those whose time and energy are consumed with making provisions for their children all too often never have the time to really get to know their children, and vice-versa.

I have always thought it would have been nice to get to know my parents, but I am afraid my opportunity has passed. I have not lived in the same state with my parents since I was 18 years old. As my parents were consumed by the responsibilities of raising eight children, I am consumed by the economic responsibility of raising a child whose father does not contribute to the child's care. I regret that I am forty years old and my parents know little about me except what they choose to see. I am simply the image they choose to hold of one of the daughters they raised. I hope my son will not grow to make the same comment about me.

I grew up in a house with both parents and yet without them. Instead, my childhood was consumed with books—The Little Princess and the Pea, Tom Thumb, Langston Hughes, Aladdin and his Magic Lamp, Hiawatha, Aesop's fables, Robinson Crusoe, The First Book of Science series, The First Book of Black History series, Old Yeller, Big Red, and the Old Woman who lived in a shoe who had so many children she did not know what to do. The Book of Knowledge Encyclopedia was my very best childhood friend and companion. I extend my undying gratitude to the authors who put it together, be they black, white, purple, yellow or blue. I had but to take the volumes off the shelf, put my fingers on the pages and they came instantly to life.

My friends in these books were always there when I needed comforting and never failed to give me a lift, whether I was reading the fairy tales so despised by the *Black Man's Guide* or reading about the latest imaginings of some rocket scientist. Real or unreal, these images sustained me at a time when my parents were overwhelmed with the responsibility of raising a family and my community was busy preparing for the revolution that never came.

My son's childhood has also been consumed by books. I bought him his first set of encyclopedias at a secondhand store when he was three years old, the summer his father and I divorced, in part because I feared the distance between us would grow. I simply could not always be there when he needed me and at the same time keep a roof over our heads and provide for his education. The books have served him well. In the third grade, my son could read at a fifth grade level. At age fifteen, he spends more time reading books than he does talking to me.

However, sometimes I am overcome with melancholy thinking that I might not know my son very well. His childhood passed so quickly, and I was always busy. The legacy of struggling to survive, like the idea that the revolution will come soon to save us, passes from generation to generation. At age 40, I am still struggling to survive and the revolution has yet to come to set me free. I suspect it never will.

Chapter 2

Reflections on the Teenage Years

The "standard process" by which the black female is taught to oppose the black male, a process which the *Black Man's Guide* informs us "does not vary much from household to household,"⁹ took a strange twist in our household during my teen years. Instead of being taught how to manipulate black males, we were totally separated from them. This was the experience of thousands of black females from strict southern Baptist and Fundamentalist homes. We were not allowed to date or go to parties, lest we turn into bad girls. Girls who dared to sit with boys at church were considered "fast." Sex was never discussed except when some bad girl "got her hook hung." We were then reminded that if we associated with boys, we would be next to get pregnant and disgrace our families. For some reason, boys who had sex before marriage were not perceived as a disgrace to the family.

Curiously, my brothers were given more freedom than ever in their teen years. They seldom came straight home from school and frequently came home late. Their so-called girlfriends were viewed as a sign of approaching maturity and given a wink and a nod. When the black males in our household brought home bad report cards or got into trouble at school, we frequently heard my parents lament that boys will be boys. If you restrict them like girls, they will turn out to be sissies. However, if a female child had dared to stay out late or not come straight home from school, she would have been whipped with a strap, the cat-o-nine-tails we used to call it. It was the same strap used by the old masters. This double standard in my parent's home was my first taste of the double standards so common to the American way of life.

For many young black girls in the South, big-city ghettos where pimps paraded up and down the streets in fancy cars and flashy jewelry, and where prostitutes flaunted themselves like gypsy moths on every lighted street corner were as foreign as Paris, France, if not more so. We could always pick up a book and read about Paris, but there was little written about the black ghettos of America.

In spite of our common poverty and oppression, the housing projects with which we were familiar did not begin to touch the human misery and degradation of the massive big-city housing projects like the Red Hook section of Brooklyn or the Cabrini Green projects in Chicago. At least the wonders of nature such as trees, grass, flowers, singing birds, ant hills, bumblebees, fresh air and fishing ponds had not been taken from us. We had no way to make comparisons, however.

We knew as little of their world of concrete as they knew of our world of unwritten rules. Emmett Till could survive in their world but in ours, he was lost.

Most of us had never been outside the state in which we were born. We knew nothing of vacations. We knew straps, harsh discipline, and the paths to school and church. If a neighbor called the house and said we were seen misbehaving, we were whipped even before being given a chance to explain. Heaven forbid the teacher or principal should call to complain. We worked hard; were respectful of our schools, communities, and elders; and received decent grades. However, to the world we were still niggers, somehow less worthy than white people no matter how hard or diligently we worked. Wherever blacks live or whatever we do, we have one universal bond—nigger. Lest we forget, there is always someone to remind us.

Twenty years and six states later, I received a harsh reminder of my American heritage just last year at a jewelry store in Westwood, California. First, I must explain that law school has been one of the most stressful and contradictory experiences of my life. The atmosphere is stifling. Sometimes I feel I am being strangulated by the contradiction between the world I know and world I must acknowledge to survive scholastically.

I was in the middle of the law school exam period when I decided to go shopping to relieve some stress and anxiety. I operate on a weird reward system: when I feel that I am at the end of my rope, I buy myself something beautiful in order to make me forget my troubles for a while. Usually I buy African art or jewelry. Often when I feel depressed, I sit and admire the beauty in small creations such as a beaded bracelet or a wood carving. With the African art, I try to imagine its creator and what his or her life was like.

Because I was experiencing an all-time low, I decided to buy something beautiful that I could carry with me throughout the day and look at and touch at my leisure. I took the bus to a jewelry store to buy a small trinket. When I rang the buzzer at the jewelry store, no one opened the door. I saw at least 3 people in the store so I rang again. Finally an old, white-haired, white man with a reddish face and a paunch came to the door and said that entry was by appointment only. I was familiar with several appointment-only stores in New York City but generally they were expensive furriers. Curious about what was in the store, I peeped in the window, hoping to see the Star of India or some other exotic delight. Strangely, I saw no truly remarkable jewelry.

I was a bit perplexed, but continued on my way to the bus stop because my exams were never far from my mind. When I passed a pay phone, the little man inside my head whispered, "Why don't you call the store and double-check." So I did. A pleasant woman named JoAnn answered the phone. Without telling her that I had just visited the store, I told her that I was interested in buying a piece of jewelry and was concerned that I might need an appointment. She assured me that no appointment was necessary for entry into the store. I walked back to the store and rang the buzzer. A middle-aged white woman named JoAnn came to the door and told me the store was closed for inventory. I was livid! I could feel the hot lava just waiting to erupt if I were not given a satisfactory explanation for what the hell was happening.

When I told her I was the woman who had just spoken with her on the phone and reminded her that she had invited me to the store, she could only utter, "You're the woman I spoke with on the phone," and stare at the ground. Through the telephone, she could not tell what color I was.

For the next five minutes, the volcano erupted and the lava spewed forth. JoAnn never said one word. She did not even look at me. She just stood there, staring at the ground. When I walked away from the store, my hands were shaking and I was sick to my stomach. I had not been that angry in years. I did not calm down until the next day. I was enraged with the assumption that blacks had no business in the store.

I was also angry with myself. I had almost forgotten that no matter where I went in life or what I did, I was still a nigger, somehow less worthy than a person with white skin. I was angry that for a moment, I had almost accepted the first bogus excuse that store entry was open by appointment only. I wanted to believe that the old white man was telling the truth. I had almost walked completely away, trusting that a white stranger had told me the truth. But a nagging doubt had pushed me to call and double-check.

The real insult came the following week when I had an attorney call the store to demand an explanation of the owner. The owner of the store admitted that his employees had given phoney excuses, but said that his store had been robbed twice that week, in fact that very morning, and that I looked suspicious. He said that his employees were only trying to protect his merchandise. Obviously black equals suspicious.

A subsequent check of the police blotter by a newspaper reporter, revealed that the owner of the store had not been truthful about the robberies.[10] There had been one attempted robbery that week by 3 black male teenagers. The week before the attempted robbery, when entry had been granted to a *white* woman, who rang the store buzzer and subsequently let 3 black men in their early 20's in the door behind her, the store had been robbed. Ironically, no black woman nor any middle-aged person like me had been involved in either incident and yet I, a 40-year-old black woman, was denied entry to the store because I looked "suspicious."

The ultimate irony was that the store owner was Jewish. Of all people, he should have known what it felt like to be singled out because one is different. The hatred I felt in my heart for him still has not gone away. Nothing would give me greater pleasure than for his store to burn to the ground, but I have too much to lose to be the one to light the match.

For months I dreamed of smashing the owner's head in, but my attorney warned me to stay away from the store and I knew that with only one more year of law school ahead of me, I had too much to lose to act on impulse. However, the murderous rage I felt scared me. I have no doubt that if JoAnn had opened the door, I would have spit in her face, not only because of her act, but because of the 40 years of rage and frustration that have built up inside of me because of the acts of white people like her. They have been killing the spirits of people of color for too long now.

Most of my friends told me to forget it, that it was not worth getting upset in the middle of exams, but I could not forget and have not forgotten. There comes a point when one can no longer just walk away. Unfortunately I can only strike back by filing a costly law suit, as most racist whites well know. If there were a world where there are no double standards, I would leave for there tomorrow. As I grow older, it becomes more and more difficult for me to hold in the anger.

When I was a teenager, the double standard that functioned in my parents' home between male and female children was portentous of the ominous double bind that lay waiting to suck black females into the gaping maw and the depths of despair when we reached maturity as blacks and as women. Somehow we knew that for us, the future held only songs of sorrow. But in our teenage years, we were too young and trusting to appreciate the subtleties.

I cannot help wondering if women, be they black or white, who are taught to scam on men to get what they want in life are not better prepared to cope with the hazards of being women in a patriarchal and racist society. It is surely safer to proceed in an indirect fashion when there are so many hands and feet waiting to slap and kick one down if one proceeds in a direct fashion. Equal opportunity has proven to be a tricky, cunning and illusive bastard.

Unlike the black mothers in the *Black Man's Guide*, my mother was spared having to deceive my father by lying about shopping trips during my teenage years because there were few shopping sprees. Because she was a teacher, my mother had summers off from her job but the work at home never abated. After the sixth grade, she taught us (the girls) to make all of our own clothes. During summers, we also made quilts and helped our mother with canning fruits and vegetables from my father's garden. Sometimes we helped at my father's garden. Hollywood movies and true romance magazines were not in our budget. Comic books were regarded as trash; therefore, we were not allowed to read them. The black girls in our household had to explain every act. There was no allowance and little trust.

We were constantly admonished to keep our dresses down, our guards up, ourselves in check and to conform to endless rules and rituals, lest we turn into the kind of women that no black man would want. Evidently, we failed to redeem ourselves since currently, only one of the five daughters has a husband. Though we live in different states and I seldom see my brother-in-law, I am truly proud to call my sister's husband my brother. His extraordinary dedication to his family is truly admirable.

As for my three blood brothers, two have been through failed marriages, and the third usually dates white women. This no doubt correlates with the position taken in the *Black Man's Guide* that the black man's biggest problems are the white man and the black woman. Nothing is ever the black man's fault and criticizing him is blasphemy. He cannot make progress only because the white man and the black woman are always plotting against him. Even his most irresponsible and reprehensible acts are not open to discussion because such discussion might make him look bad in the eyes of the world, as if Madison Avenue public relations gimmicks can eradicate racism in America.

There is, however, one final permutation on the obstacles-facing-black-males argument that also merits consideration, i.e., that black men are also disadvantaged because black men plot against each other. Recently in Los Angeles, when Bob Gay (a black male) lost the ninth District City Council seat to Rita Walters (a black female), who was backed by Mayor Tom Bradley (himself a black man), the tearful Gay commented, "The mayor has never been a great promoter of young black males."[11] Although only one with his or her eyes closed to reality (or blinded by the heavy scales of justice) could contend that ours is a color-blind society and that black males are not discriminated against on a daily basis, it seems absurd to argue that the black mayor of Los Angeles does not support black males. Is the shield that was designed to protect the disadvantaged to become the sword used to strike down the very disadvantaged it was designed to protect? Is it not peculiar that those who readily acknowledge that one black man will turn on another find it incomprehensible that the same black man who readily turns on his brother will also turn on his sister, the black woman, who is an easier target?

The usual arguments related to plotting against the black man, however, generally revolve around the deceitful black female plotting against the black male. If only this treacherous creature would take a back seat and stop scamming on the black male, he could get the support he needs to succeed, or so the story goes. Interestingly, as suggested in the *Black Man's Guide*, the black woman is frequently noted for taking sides with her family against her black husband.

However, the loyalty of the white woman to her newly acquired mate, whose family is not only often against her liaison with a black male but also of a completely different race, the very race who implemented slavery in America, is never questioned. Unlike Sapphire, the white woman can accept the black man for his true worth. The white woman's wisdom and her loyalty to the black man is so great that she, unlike Sapphire, is able to resist and overcome society's conditioning against the black male, the very barrier on which the stubborn and recalcitrant Sapphire constantly bumps her hard head.

The speculation continues that unlike the cunning and conniving black woman who is responsible for the downfall of the black race, the white woman is an innocent victim of the white man's duplicity and deceit. The white man has turned her children into uncaring and unfeeling racists, in spite of his touted preoccupation with work and noted frequent absence from the home due to his putting in long hours at the office. Like the black woman, the white man's negative influence on his race is so strong that he has singlehandedly brought about the moral bankruptcy of his race.

Magically, when the black woman steps aside and gives the black man his rightful place in the home and community, the thereby empowered black male will conquer the weak white male, who we all know used to crawl around howling in caves but only jumped bad after he invented the bullet, or so the story goes. Unlike the host of professionally and economically successful black men sporting white women on their arms today, the newly empowered black man will instead bring the black woman to the throne with him.

Though the *Black Man's Guide* derides black women for exposing their children to fairy tales, the author presents the conquering black knight fairy tale as a real life scenario rather than the fairy tale which it is. When a white man says the white woman is loyal and virtuous but the black woman is cunning and deceitful, we quickly label him a racist. When a black man makes the same statement, we say the brother has a point about Sapphire. If the black woman dares to criticize the black male, we quickly label her divisive and the reason the black male has so many problems. That the black woman is responsible for the downfall of the black male, but the white woman is an innocent victim of the acts perpetrated by the white male is fundamentally illogical.

If a black woman were to write a black female's guide to the black male that portrayed the black male as he is typically stereotyped—lazy and shiftless, lacking in character and common sense, and needing to be trained as one would train a dog—the stink raised would reach the heavens. In his essay in response to the *Black Man's Guide*, *Ultimate Confusion: A Black Woman's Self-Hatred*, Haki Madhubuti cleverly transcribed an excerpt from the *Black Man's Guide* switching the feminine designations to masculine designations to illustrate this very point:

> Since he is such a pseudo romantic creature he cannot be trusted in the presence of strange women for a long length of time because he is always open for a line, especially if it's one telling him how handsome or desirable he is. He believes anything a Blackwoman tells him if she looks good to him physically.
>
> He brags on his sexual conquests in the same way the Blackwoman is rumored to brag about hers. He will explain to his friends in great detail about his activities in bed with a Blackwoman. He especially likes to tell about the size of her vagina, what she says while copulating, her stroke and whether or not she performed oral sex as well. They go into a minute by minute, blow by blow description about the encounter. If she does any oddities he calls her nasty and other horrible names and he and his friends laugh at her. It is a rare Blackman who does not tell about his private sexual life with a Blackwoman.[12]

No doubt those men who found this passage amusing when the black female bore the brunt of the stigma are no longer laughing when they are the object of the character assassination. This is not surprising in light of the response to the movie *The Color Purple*.

The hue and cry raised over the movie, *The Color Purple*, is a good example of the precarious predicament of the black woman. The acting, script, and cast were excellent. However, Whoopi Goldberg and Alice Walker were berated by black males for bringing up a "sensitive" topic, the black man and rape. Alice Walker did not invent black rape or sex abuse and the white man has not been the only rapist of black women in America. Much to my sorrow, one of my own brothers was convicted of the assault with intent to rape of his stepdaughter several years after the movie premiered. Thus the problem of black-on-black rape still exists for black women and girls in America. Whether we are too ashamed or embarassed to admit it, many of us have been touched by rape in one way or another. Rape is not something that happens only to

33

the bad women down the street, nor is rape perpetrated only by the bad men down the street. Rape, symptomatic of the universal oppression of women, is part and parcel of our social fabric.

The rape of black women is not the infrequent act of a few deviant black men. The rape of black women by black men is a daily occurrence. In spite of the large numbers of rapes that go unreported, the police blotters across America tell the stories of the thousands of women who are raped. Those blacks who deny the rape of the black woman at the hands of the black man are no different from those whites who insist that we live in a color-blind society and that discrimination is only the infrequent act of a few deviant white men. The willful blindness of both is just plain dangerous in light of the large numbers of those who continue to be victimized and oppressed.

Society's obsession with the rape of white women by black men completely overlooks the fact that far more black women have been raped by black men than have white women, and that many of these black women (and girls) were raped in their own homes. Because of white society's murderous preoccupation with even the possibility of the rape of white women by black males, the loyal black woman is expected to stand silently by and deny her own rape at the hand of black males. Just as she is expected to sacrifice her economic interests for "the good of the race," the black woman is now supposed to sacrifice her interest in her own body for "the good of the race." It is utmost perversity that white men are known for killing black men for even looking at white women, but black men would deny black women the right to express outrage at the violation of their own bodies!

How long must black women tie their guts into knots and bite their tongues almost clear through, to correct problems created by whites? Why blame the victim? Black women have suffered long enough for problems that we did not create. Black men should direct their anger at the source of the problem instead of at us!

It is unfortunate that many innocent black men have lost their lives because of false cries of rape by some white women, but if the numerous black men whom we see dating and marrying white women are content to "forgive and forget," and are obviously not worried about the historically disparate treatment of black men by the legal system when it comes to the rape of white women, why should the burden for what "has" happened or "might" happen to the black man at the hands of racist whites fall on the backs of black women? Black women are not only subject to rape themselves by both black men and white men, but also have been the victims of rape far more often than white women. Black women certainly have not raped anyone! And, few *if any* men, black or white, have ever been lynched for the rape of a black woman because society has not concerned itself with the rape of the so-called "immoral" or "licentious" black Sapphire or Jezebel! Why should the black woman continue to suffer in silence because of the acts of white women or white men or black men in the sorry history of this country?

The history is sorry indeed! Between 1930 and 1967, 36 percent of the black men who were convicted of raping a white woman were executed.[13] In stark contrast, only 2 percent of all defendants convicted of rape involving other racial combinations, were executed.[14] Even today, black men convicted of raping white women receive longer prison sentences than other rape defendants.[15] However, muzzling the black woman is not the solution to this problem.

Society's selective acknowledgement of the seriousness of the rape of white women by black men has been accompanied by a denial of the rape of black women, by black and white men, that began in slavery and continues today.[16] Because of racism and sexism, little has been written about this denial. The racists, like the sexists, refuse to acknowledge the problem.

The predicament of the black female slave was sadly illustrated in the case of *George, a Slave, v. State*, 37 Mississippi 306 (1859). There, the Mississippi Supreme Court dismissed the indictment of a male slave for the rape of a female slave less than ten years old, reasoning "that Masters and slaves can not be governed by the same system or laws; so different are their positions, rights and duties." The following year the state legislature outlawed the attempted or actual rape of a black or mulatto female under age twelve by a black or mulatto male. See, 1860 Miss. Laws 62. However, the legislature refused to recognize the rape of adult black females, by black or white males, and the rape of any black females by white men.[17]

Our legal system has rendered the rape of black women by any man invisible, like much of the history of the black woman. These attitudes reflect a set of myths about black women's supposed promiscuity, i.e., women who are not "chaste" cannot be raped. Even today, the claims of black rape victims are taken less seriously than those of white victims.[18] Ironically, black women are more likely to be victims of rape than are white women.[19] Based on data from national surveys of rape victims, "the profile of the most frequent rape victim is a young woman, divorced or separated, black and poverty stricken."[20] And yet this sister is supposed to keep her mouth shut about rape because of this country's historic mistreatment of the black male. Once again, the experience of the black male is deemed more important than the experience of the black female. Why?

Once again, the black female is expected to suffer in silence, "for the greater good of the black race," because of the sexist assumption that men's experiences are more important than women's experiences and that what matters most among men's experiences is their ability to assert themselves patriarchally. The black male thus must be allowed to reign as the noble patriarch in his family like the white man, which means that the rape of black women is to remain inconsequential.

It is more important that the black man be allowed to assert himself and be spared the embarrassment of his own foul deeds than to free the black woman of the fear of rape. After all, it is only rape and she should be used to it by now! No consideration is given to the predicament in which this places the black woman. She is just supposed to be grateful that the black man is free to assert himself, and be glad to take her place behind him. If she is a good girl, her man will protect her, i.e., if he is around when some other man decides to assert his right to rape her.

Unfortunately for the black woman, most rapists are smart enough to wait until the husband is not around, just as most racists are smart enough not to announce that niggers are not allowed. Even the dumbest rapists have figured that part out. Now for the sister who is not attached to some man who can protect her, life is tough. Perhaps she should take in a brother who is fooling around on the side. After all, half a man is better than none, or so the story goes.

This is not unlike the game played on white women by white men. The moral of the story is usually that a woman had better behave herself and submit to the authority of some man so that she will have a man to protect her in the jungle of life. Otherwise, God only knows what could happen to her. The story is a thousand years old, submission for protection, as long as the woman does not get old and fat, because then hubby might be tempted to run off with some sweet young thing who is much more in need of his protection. Of course if hubby is old and decrepit, too, he will not be able to fight like he used to, but chances are the years have been good to hubby and he can buy all of the protection his sweetie needs, whether it is a gun (lower class), an elaborate burglar alarm system (middle class), or a body guard (upper class). Hubby will do anything for "the lady of the house."

If being "the lady of the house" means that I, as a black woman, must sit by silently and watch my husband (or any other man) abuse any black woman (or white woman), just so that my economic needs will be taken care of, then I for one will struggle alone. I am not that desperate yet. If the legacy of slavery has taught me anything, it is that silence is a crime. Those who were silent about the capture and enslavement of a race of people, those who were silent about the rapes and lynchings, those who were silent about the daily torture and torment were just as guilty as those who threw up the ropes. Likewise, those who are silent today about the oppression of black women are just as guilty as those who oppress black women, be the oppressor black or white.

36

I cringe to think of all the white "ladies of the house" who sat by while my great-great-grandmothers and great-great-great-grandmothers were raped and abused. I cringe to think of all the white people who could have helped my ancestors, but instead sat silently. My fraternal great-great-grandparents continued to work as slaves even after the Civil War was over because they could not read or write and no one told them the war was over and that they were free. One whispered word by one kind soul would have alerted them to their freedom after years of abuse, but no one spoke until a stranger who rode into town on a mule spoke. My ancestors then moved from Georgia to Texas. It is a pity that they did not keep moving farther west, but with the little or nothing they had, I suppose they were pretty fortunate to get as far as Texas. So strong was my desire to get the hell out of Texas that I left Texas three days after graduating from high school.

Because of the history of the tremendous suffering of my people, I cannot stand idly by while anyone is abused. I know the cruelty of silence. Often it hurts worse than the lash. At least by the lash one knows the enemy.

In spite of what was written in the Constitution of the United States of America, the enslavement of blacks was a crime against humanity and nature. In spite of what was written in the law books, the rape of black women was wrong 300 years ago and is wrong today. Black women have no choice except to speak out about rape or any other abuse, whether the rapist or abuser is black or white because if we do not speak, who will? Our oppressors will not speak, be they black or white, because we are an embarrassment to them. They would rather forget us. Unless we speak out, we, the most likely victims, will continue to be victimized. If history has taught us anything, it is that our condition will not change unless we change it ourselves. As one who has also been a victim of rape, I will not stand silently by while black women are abused merely so that black men will enjoy a good reputation in the white community.

Black men who are angered at the black male/white female rape myth should direct their anger at the source of the problem instead of targeting black women for seeking justice when wronged. Black women are just as tired of the legacies and burdens of slavery as black men, if not more so, as black women were the slaves of slaves. Reasoning that the black woman should keep her mouth shut about rape to protect the black male's image is clearly flawed, similar to the flawed reasoning in much of the *Black Man's Guide*.

The reasoning presented in the *Black Man's Guide* related to male-female relationships lacks even common sense. Anyone who can count knows that all black women can never be paired with a black mate any more than all white women can be paired with a white mate because there are more women than men in both races. Therefore many women who make no plans other than to "catch a man" will meet the fate of the little grasshopper who spent the entire summer enjoying the sun's rays but froze to death when jack frost came because he had made no preparations for winter. Those who assure us that every woman can find a man cleverly avoid the issue of what happens to the women who do not, or who are abused by the men they do find and must leave the relationship.

What I would like to know is what happens to the black woman that no black man wants, the legendary sisters like Caldonia and Lucille with hard heads and big feet, who have been made immortal by blues singers and black comedians? The big black sister with short kinky hair, thick lips, and big feet may be just as anxious to get married as her petite, light-skinned, white-looking counterpart with the shoulder-length silky mane. Of course since the dark sister is not considered fine or "dope," as the rapper's say, she is always second or third choice in the meat market, whether the male shopper is looking for a date or a mate. Is Sapphire to fall off the face of the earth simply because the brothers consider her undesirable?

As an adult, when I lived in New York City and rode the subway daily, hardly a day passed that I did not hear a group of young inner-city black males discussing their female conquests. They were very proud of their conquests and spoke loudly enough for all to hear, black or white. I was dismayed at how often I heard the comment, "Man, that bitch is too black fo' me! I cain't dee-al with no ug-a-ly black bitch." At this point the commenter and his cohorts would break into laughter slapping their thighs, grabbing their crotches, and making various other derisive remarks. The scenario was always the same, disgusting and disheartening.

Even before the advent of interracial dating, the black man's preference for light-skinned women was obvious. Though I have never made an official body count, I cannot help noticing that most black men marry women of a lighter complexion than themselves. This was true of my maternal and fraternal grandparents' marriages, my parents' marriage, all my aunts' and uncles' marriages, and my own marriage. I have discussed this observation with black male and female friends alike and none protest that it is not so. Darker skinned females are clearly at a disadvantage in the selection process.

As a child, I remember most vividly leafing through *Jet* and *Ebony* marvelling at all the beautiful light-skinned women, wondering how they got their hair to look so soft and straight. Almost forty years later, little about the black women on the pages of these magazines (or about the men who select them) has changed, except that I no longer marvel at their beauty. Instead, I marvel at the fortitude of any particularly dark-skinned female who aspires to the stage, screen, or theater. Like the black woman who aspires to be a housewife, she too is bucking stiff odds, and is likely to experience a hard fall no matter how talented she is.

As an adult, I remember most vividly my son's eight-year-old summer playmates in New York City, a large number of whom were black and Puerto Rican, running to the gate to greet me after school and expressing their surprise that I was not dark like my son. I am not particularly light-skinned but my son is very dark-skinned like his father. Once I explained to the children that my son's father, whom they had never seen, was very dark, the questions about skin color ceased. I know that the children did not mean any harm, but the whole process was annoying and vexatious to my son, so much so that he once expressed his dismay at being dark like his dad. Even as I lectured to my son that skin color should not make a difference, I knew that such was not the case.

The process was also a bit curious in that my son's playmates at the predominantly white schools he had previously attended never questioned the difference in his color and mine. The young white student's confusion usually centered on things like why the inside of my son's and my palms and the bottom of our feet were white, but the rest of our skin was black. Like their adult counterparts, children too are color struck, even black children.

In our color-struck society, reality for black women is that no female actresses the color of Wesley Snipes are portrayed as beautiful *or talented* by the black or white media. Yet what has skin color to do with the ability to act out a drama? Why should dark skin be correlated with lack of talent, or is it that the audience only wants to see those things presented that it aspires to, and dark skin is not an aspirational goal?

On a past Christmas vacation with my son to the Soviet Union, I was struck by the influence of color consciousness on even those who make an effort to guard against this ugly monster. Six of us (Americans—including one judge and two attorneys) attended a performance of *Swan Lake* and when a Chinese prima ballerina flitted gracefully and effortlessly onto the stage filled with an all white troupe, all of us, both black and white, picked up our binoculars in unison, like precisely programmed clones, to make sure we saw what we thought we saw. Though none of us admitted it, all of us were surprised to see a performance with a mixed cast, especially among those playing the lead roles. And yet, what difference did it make? Only the oddity of American racial practices, and our acceptance of them, caused us to do a double-take on seeing a Chinese prima ballerina dance *Swan Lake*.

She was very beautiful and extremely talented, so much so that she had to come out for several curtain calls. The audience simply would not let her go. No one appeared to notice that the prima ballerina was "different" except the six Americans in the audience.

Unfortunately in our color-struck society, the too big, too black, too strong teenage female never metamorphoses into Tchaikovsky's beautiful swan in the eyes of the black or white community. Sapphire can never be the swan. She remains the ugly duckling. For her, adulthood is equally as painful, if not more so, than the teenage years.

What happens to the rejected black women that no one wants? Do we forget them because they are an embarrassment or an unpleasant reminder that there but for the grace of God go I? Who is to take care of the rejected women and their children? Are they like lemmings to cast themselves into the sea because they could not "catch a man?" Does the future hold anything for them but the public dole? Perhaps it is our young black teenage sisters who should proudly sport the too big, too black, too strong tee-shirts that are so popular among our black male youth. It is truly ironic that the very men who cry that America discriminates against them because they are too big, too black, and too strong employ the same discriminating tactics against black females.

Chapter 3

Reflections on Adulthood

In adulthood the black woman discovers how little she is valued even in her own community. I once heard my father comment upon learning that a crippled black woman confined to a wheelchair married a caring black man who was not crippled, "Why on earth did he marry her? What good is a woman who can't serve a man?" Like the notion that blacks were put on earth to serve whites, the notion that women were put on earth to serve men survives. Sadly, this notion is perpetuated by the black church, where artificial role distinctions are encouraged for no reason other than "the Bible says so."

Whites who promoted segregation "because the Bible says so" saw themselves just as dutiful to the word of God as the Bible thumping black ministers who readily impose all kinds of restrictions on black women in the name of Jesus Christ. For both, it is easier to take the stance that one is directed by God, therefore not subject to question, and cling to mindless tradition rather than question why the burden falls where it does. In many black churches today, black women are not allowed in the pulpit except to read church announcements or play the organ. A black woman who cannot afford stockings for herself and her girls would not dream of going to a black church bare-legged for she knows such behavior would be totally unacceptable, even though in many black churches women are not allowed to wear pants to cover their legs.

I will never forget the time I took off from work and travelled hundreds of miles with my then-husband and our teething baby through a Midwest snowstorm to attend my husband's grandmother's funeral only to be turned away from the church because I was wearing pants. The church was in the midst of a large inner-city urban ghetto. The temperature outside hovered at a few degrees above zero, the wind was blowing like the hawk, and the sidewalks in front of the church were glazed with ice and snow.

I watched in awe as old black women who could walk only with the assistance of canes stumbled through the snow and navigated up the slippery church steps in short skirts and high heel shoes. The wind-chill factor was well below zero and the legs of these old women must have been freezing. They moved so slowly they looked like cardboard statues being blown by the wind. They held on to each other since few of them had a man to assist them. No doubt they viewed themselves as brave women trusting in the Lord to take care of them while they were about

His business. Actually, they appeared quite foolish in their skirts and heels in spite of their good intentions. Thoughts of my friends who had broken bones in their old age and never healed right flashed through my mind. These old women easily could have met a similar fate treading the icy pavement, and yet the church's only concern was that these sisters come to church "looking like women." Such shallow and superficial thinking continues to result in burdens being imposed on black women!

Strangely, the black women in the black church continue to bow down in submission to every requirement imposed and accept their lot, in spite of the fact that black women outnumber black men in the church by at least two to one. Without black women and their hard-earned money, there would be no black church! In spite of the subservient role black women have assumed in the black church, black women have been and continue to be the backbone of the black churches that by official decree can be run only by black men.

There are few places in life where the minority rules the majority. South Africa is one such place, the black church is another. Ironically, those who easily see the oppression of the minority regime in South Africa cannot see the oppression of the minority regime in the black church. In both institutions, men rule by "divine right" and those who dare to challenge are banished. Perhaps someday the women in the black church will rise and claim what is rightfully theirs.

It has always gnawed at my guts to watch the old black women who clean white people's houses for a living put their hard-earned dollars in the church so that a black man who seldom sweats outside the pulpit can wear fancy clothes, drive a luxury automobile, and bring back reports from the white community that the old hard-working sisters know only through the back door or the kitchen. It seems that in this world, everyone wants to have a king and will pay for it dearly, be the king the bonnie Prince Charlie or the good Reverend Doctor. And yet when these meek and submissive women leave the church, suddenly they become the emboldened Sapphire, the brazen, bossy and domineering bitches who have never learned how to stand behind a black man and thereby make life hell for the brothers. Once again, black women cannot win for losing.

As I watched the old women blow like cardboard in the breeze on their way to the funeral, the minister of the church arrived. Ironically, the elegantly tailored minister was wearing a big, bulky coat of a cloth so heavy that clothing manufacturers do not use it for women's coats, in spite of the warmth the cloth provides. (Women are limited in the selection of their clothing because manufacturers assume it is more important for women to be fashionable rather than functional.) His heavy coat fell well below his knees and his flat sturdy shoes allowed him to plant his feet firmly on the pavement. The minister had a flock of deacons to assist him up the steps when he got out of his Cadillac, lest harm befall the valued leader who had travelled a good distance to reach his ghetto church that blustery Chicago morning. Like many affluent black ministers, he lived far out in a white suburban community rather than in the dangerous westside Chicago ghetto in which it was his parishioners' misfortune to live. He also had a summer home in a small town in rural Michigan where blacks were safe because they were still a novelty. The loyal parishioners could look at their affluent minister and dream that the good Lord would bless them someday so that they too could move out into suburban paradise with the rich white folks, away from the notorious Chicago gangs and the fierce hawk. Until then, they remained obedient servants. The minister has long since died, and most of the loyal parishioners who are still alive are still trapped in the same westside ghetto into which they were born.

For many years, every time I visited Chicago, my first stop was the westside. It seldom occurred to me that it was a so-called dangerous ghetto. I always made a trip to Green's Barbecue on the westside and hit a few local westside bee-bop bars with friends to hear the latest and watch the dancers bop. No one could bop like the sisters from Chicago, though the sisters from Gary, Indiana, and East St. Louis, Illinois, came close. Even though I was raised in the land of beef and brew—Texas—I readily conceded that westside Chicago had the best barbecue and bartenders in the world. The best friend I ever had still lives on the westside in the same neighborhood she lived in 20 years ago when she took me in, but I no longer go there. My visits with her and her daughter are limited to phone calls.

Even the ghettos are not like they used to be since the invention of crack. The bartenders who used to give us drinks for free just to keep a good crowd in the house now have hearts as cold and hard as the steel bars that cover every door and window. The men who used to buy a drink for every lady in the house so that no woman would dare to turn down a request for a dance are no more. Besides, it is no longer safe to accept drinks compliments of a stranger, as the stranger is liable to come to the table and demand more than a dance.

The care-free weekends when we headed straight for the ghetto if one were within one hundred miles, the only place we really felt accepted, are gone forever. Hanging out was perhaps a frivolous activity for young adults, but nowadays, with crack and drive-by shootings, hanging out is just plain dangerous. Even concerts are plagued by violence and one never knows if the gang members in the audience, who care little whether anyone enjoys the concert besides themselves, will decide to march in the aisles or across the stage.

43

I have been more fortunate than the many people I know who remain trapped in ghettos. I have travelled freely in and out of many ghettos as an adult, but have never been trapped there. For me, there was always a ready exit. However, my upbringing in the South was not unlike the upbringing of my cohorts in the big city ghettos in many ways.

For instance, the minister of the church in which I was raised was not much different from the ghetto minister at my ex-husband's grandmother's funeral. I lost all respect for the minister of the church in which I was raised when he told one of the young women in the church who managed to graduate from a theological seminary that he could give her a good recommendation so that she could go to another church but that he could not allow her in his pulpit because the church was not ready for it. He would have been kinder to spit in her face.

How many black men have related a similar story as to why they were denied a promotion or a job by a white man? How many thought the white man's actions could be justified? Why should any woman who will not accept second-class treatment because of her race accept second-class treatment because of her sex? Those who condemn the white man for keeping his foot on the backs of blacks, while at the same time keeping their feet on the backs of women are hypocrites of the worst variety, be they black or white!

Though he has taken most of the heat, the white man has not been the only chauvinist pig in America. Black women dare not criticize the black man lest they be called the divisive Sapphire. White women dare not criticize black men lest they be called racists. Therefore the black male has been allowed to reap the benefits of sexism while protesting his innocence. Contrary to what many believe, sexist oppression has little to do with one's bank roll or portfolio. The poorest man in America can be just as oppressive of the women in his world as the richest.

Those black women in America who are not afraid of being branded traitors can readily testify as to how easily the oppressed become the oppressors when given unbridled authority, and to the number of ways that black women are oppressed. Few men or women openly challenge or question the condition of black women. It is easier to accept tradition mindlessly than to question where the burdens imposed by those traditions fall. This is true in both the white and black communities as my experiences in non-traditional fields have shown me.

Before going into law, I spent 12 years working as a journeyman electrician for the International Brotherhood of Electrical Workers. The Local in which I served my apprenticeship had never had a black or a woman member in its 100-year existence, as was true of most of the building trades in the town. In spite of the fact that I scored as high as it was possible to score in all 3 designated areas of the written examination, I was bumped as a result of the oral interview. At the interview, I was asked questions about baby-sitting problems and was privileged to sit and listen to the interviewers debate whether their wives could do the work. I could have been a block of wood for all it mattered.

After I hired an attorney, the committee reconsidered my application and invited me to start work, a month behind the other apprentices in my class. I found out later that bets were taken as to how long I would last on the job. The lone young white male on the job who had bet on me informed me that he did not want to lose his money. Frequently, derogatory remarks were written on the job-site walls about blacks. The inside of the port-o-johns were filled with drawings of me, the "uppity black bitch," and what should be done to me to straighten me out. The frequent comments that I needed a "real man" to set me straight were a strange precursor of the warnings in the *Moynihan Report* related to the "tangled Negro pathology" and the dangerous black "matriarchy."

According to Moynihan, "[a] fundamental fact of Negro American family life is the often reversed roles of husband and wife."[21] Furthermore, because the matriarchal structure:

> ...is so out of line with the rest of the American society, [it] seriously retards the progress of the group as a whole, and imposes a crushing burden on the Negro male...[22]
> ...[M]ost Negro youth are in *danger* of being caught up in the tangle of pathology that affects their world...[23] ...[A]t the center of the tangle of pathology is the weakness of the family structure. Once or twice removed, it will be found to be the principal source of most of the aberrant, inadequate, or anti-social behavior that did not establish, but now serves to perpetuate the cycle of poverty and deprivation.[24]
> ...[I]n a society that measures a man by the size of his paycheck, [the black man] doesn't stand very tall.... To this situation he may react with withdrawal, bitterness toward society, aggression both within the family and racial group, self-hatred or crime. Or he may escape through a number of avenues that help him to lose himself in fantasy or to compensate for his low status through a variety of exploits.[25]

Although most of my co-workers probably had never read the *Moynihan Report*, intuitively these workers reached the same conclusion about black women that Mr. Moynihan reached—somehow the black woman must be put back into her proper place. Like many people with dark skin I was accustomed to being an outsider, and I was able to endure the sense of isolation I frequently felt on the construction sites. Eventually I finished my apprenticeship.

After moving to New York City to work, I was overjoyed with the prospect that in the big city I would have the opportunity to work around black electricians and other black building trades workers, as well as other women. My joy did not last long however. There were few women (the first female to complete the grueling apprenticeship program in New York City was a white male who had a sex change operation) and most of the black men on the jobs took the attitude that I should have stayed at home so that a black man could have my job and thereby provide for his family. As far as these black men were concerned, a black woman's place was in the kitchen. And yet these men considered the white man the oppressor. I felt as oppressed by the black man as I did by the white man. Whether the foot on my throat was black or white, or whether the man stepping on me intended to or not, it still hurt.

Ironically, if I could have collected the $35/week child support that was due me, I would have made ends meet with a minimum wage job and never moved to a city where I knew no one, looking for work. However, I was desperate. When my flight landed at La Guardia, my last $278 was in my pocket as I had been out of work for quite some time. I lived in cheap hotels paying my rent by the day or the week until I could save enough to get an apartment.

Like the author of the *Black Man's Guide*, the black men I encountered assumed that any black woman who "acted right" would magically have a husband. If acting right means accepting your husband's womanizing, drug or alcohol abuse, chronic unemployment, and physical or child abuse, perhaps these men are right. However, I cannot imagine any rational woman subjecting herself to that kind of physical and mental oppression just to be with a man. In this respect, black men have been no more noble than white men. Both have oppressed women and continue to oppress women. The black woman is so oppressed that she dare not mention her oppression lest she be branded a traitor to her race for publicly criticizing the black male. This is the reality with which black women must deal. Some black females deal with harsh reality by denying it.

The mental oppression of black women struck a loud chord for me for the first time some twelve years ago. Frequently I spoke to women's groups about my experiences as a non-traditional worker. In fact we had a small female support group that consisted of a carpenter, a heavy equipment operator, an auto mechanic and an electrician. Unfortunately I was the only black member in the group. In a small town, one quickly gains a reputation, good or bad.

46

About that time, I was confronted by a black welfare mother with three children, whose mother before her had raised her family on welfare, who stated that she just could not understand what any woman would want with a man's job. I last spoke with this same woman several months ago when she expressed to me that she was depressed and wanted to get her life together, but was so overwhelmed that she did not know where to start.

After twelve years of "trying to catch a man," this same woman is sixty pounds heavier, looks twenty years older and does not know what she will do in two years when her last child becomes eighteen and the aid to dependent children checks stop coming. The father of her first two children drank himself to death at an early age. The father of her last child, who abandoned her years ago, is a drug addict who is currently in jail and has never taken much interest in their child. The child is two or three grades behind in school and is functionally illiterate. This woman lives in a large urban ghetto where she is afraid to go outside after dark. Her daughter and her daughter's three out-of-wedlock children, whose fathers also provide no support, live with her. Her daughter is also on welfare in addition to having a drug problem. One of the young grandchildren has already been sexually molested.

This same woman is paralyzed by depression. She is angry that there is no black man to rescue her from her misery. She drinks coffee all day long while watching television to soothe her jangled nerves. Sometimes she can get medication from her doctor at the clinic for her "nerves." She wants to go back to school since she never finished high school but cannot find the energy or motivation to pick up the forms. She does not want to do cleaning work and asked me for advice. I was stymied because I knew that if offered a "man's job" tomorrow that would pay her a good wage, she would not take it for fear of being unfeminine. She still hopes to meet a nice man someday who will appreciate her for her good qualities and who will take care of her. She has chosen not to face the reality of being a black woman in America. Even today, she sits and drinks coffee, paralyzed by depression.

She is not unlike some other black (and white) women in America who hold on to the American dream of the knight in shining armor who puts his woman on a pedestal. She does not want to think of the women who have had to plow fields behind a mule to survive just because they were black. She does not want to think of all the women in her neighborhood who are just like her and her mother, and like her daughter is rapidly becoming. Those thoughts get on her "nerves" and run up her blood pressure.

I experienced a similar situation in New York City when I worked on a construction project at Bronx Lebanon Hospital. Bronx Lebanon is located in one of the most notorious ghetto areas in the City. I frequently heard men and women make comments about women in construction as I walked past wearing my construction boots, hard hat and tool pouch.

Unlike other hospitals at which I had worked that were in areas populated by affluent whites, at which construction workers were not allowed to use the elevators used by the hospital's clientele to transport tools and materials, at Bronx Lebanon we frequently stopped the elevators to move our tools and materials. There was a shortage of everything at the hospital, including elevators. The emergency room personnel were swamped. Frequently we walked past dead bodies on stretchers that were waiting for processing. Dead babies, of which there were an alarming number, received immediate attention. There were so many people in the waiting rooms that the hospital kept several televisions playing all day to distract the occupants from their misery while they waited sometimes for hours. The doctors and nurses were terrific, but could do little about the tragic conditions in the community in which they worked.

Pregnant teenage girls who came for check ups brought the whole family with them, which usually included two or three toddlers with runny noses, often with dirty or wrinkled clothing, who cried incessantly. If one stopped to speak to these toddlers, they seem amazed that anyone would pay them attention. Many were too bashful to speak even if their mothers prodded them. They seemed afraid to ask questions when given the opportunity to ask, and though their eyes were riveted to our tools, they seemed somehow afraid of the tools if given the opportunity to touch them. They were perplexing and heartbreaking, bright but somehow backwards.

On occasion, the security guards had to break up fights in the emergency room that had started in the streets or home and continued or spilled over in the hospital waiting room or emergency room. When the temperature soared, the body count soared. On Monday mornings, there was always a bloody stretcher. The old women at the hospital always had tears, not for themselves but for their loved ones. Never had I seen such human misery in America. Frequently I asked myself, "How is this possible in America, the land of the free and home of the brave?" Many construction workers refused to work in the neighborhood.

Even the hospital maintenance workers were concerned with La Sida—AIDS, and the possibility of contamination. The usual handles on the plungers that the maintenance workers used to unstop toilets had been removed and replaced by handles that were five feet long, so that the workers could distance themselves from any human body fluids. It was tragic comedy to see plungers that stood tall like men wearing black boots. One could hardly laugh, as the men who used these jerry-rigged plungers were deathly afraid in spite of their machismo. They had families who depended upon them for support. No one wants to die the horrible death of AIDS. The floor moppers wore rubber gloves and sometimes masks. Rubber gloves and masks were the order of the day.

I used to think the workers overreacted until I read that subsequent anonymous and random blood testing conducted sometime after 1988, of a targeted age bracket of male patients at the hospital revealed an HIV infection rate of over 50 percent. There were no openly gay males in this neighborhood, as they probably would have been beaten to death or at least within an inch of their lives. The neighborhood was hostile to gays. To the hostile community, the scourge of poverty, drugs, crime, and prostitution was more than enough to deal with without the additional burden of homosexuality. I was one of the few construction workers at the job site who was not daily solicited by prostitutes when walking from the subway to the job site. If the hospital staff had not been more noble than the construction workers who refused to work in the neighborhood, the community would have been hard-pressed for medical services.

In the midst of all this poverty and despair, I happened to stop an elevator one day to transport a ladder and a bundle of pipe when I overheard one black pregnant teen whisper to another, "You couldn't pay me enough to do that kind of work." At the time, 1986, I was making about $1500 a week and seldom had less than $300 in my wallet, while they were at the hospital in search of free medical services. Both had their cards entitling them to free clinical services in hand because they were well acquainted with the clinic process. Although I was dressed in jeans and work boots, I lived in a beautiful three bedroom apartment on the upper westside of Manhattan and my son and I had just returned from our annual two week Christmas vacation, this time in the Virgin Islands. In spite of the fact that I worked hard for a living, I had doors opened to me of which these girls could only dream. Two years later I could afford to quit the electrical trade to attend law school.

The irony was heartbreaking. I wanted to grab them and shake them and shout, "Wake up! No one is going to save you from this hell hole!" Here were two young black teenage females, both pregnant, one with a baby in her arms; neither wearing a wedding ring; both wearing flashy but obviously cheap polyester clothing and plastic high-heeled shoes; reeking of cheap perfume (that smelled like cat piss as my ex-husband's grandmother was fond to lament); sporting fancy hair-do's and long, painted, artificial finger nails with glitter, as if they were members of the leisure class when probably they had never been outside the

49

Bronx and could not plan their lives past their next welfare checks. All that they were trained to see when looking at a woman in other than a traditional or subordinate position was that it was not cute. Working hard or sweating for a living was a crime against femininity. They were trapped as surely as if someone were holding a gun on them, but by their own thinking, the same misguided thinking presented in the *Black Man's Guide.*

I hope that my assessment of these girls (I hesitate to call them women as neither looked older than seventeen) was wrong and that both have completed their educations and are currently doctors or nurses at the hospital at which they once sought free medical services, or that both have found stable husbands who can help them provide for their babies, but I doubt it. Like most young, black, teenage mothers who get themselves trapped in this bad predicament, they are probably still on the same street corner, hoping and waiting for a black knight in shining armor who will never come, and blaming the world for their problems.

Though the world is at fault for many of their problems, the world is not at fault for their denial of reality. The influence of the Madison Avenue think tanks is mighty, but each of us still has freedom of choice (except when it comes to abortions). Those who continue to buy into the myths that are far more dangerous than believing in Santa Claus ever was, will continue to suffer for those misguided beliefs. The myth of the black knight in shining armor that books like the *Black Man's Guide* or the *Moynihan Report* or columns like William Raspberry's "To Restore the American Family, First Save the Boys" continue to hold out to these young girls is patently false. Most of the black knights these young girls are apt to meet in their neighborhoods not only will be unable to afford armor but also will be lucky to have a horse. It is difficult indeed to ride off into the sunset without a horse.

Reality for these young black women in America is ultra-harsh. They have so many miles to travel just to reach the starting block that most will give up. My heart bleeds for the young black pregnant teens who will never find a shining knight—and most will not, whether they accept the reality or not. As troubled as the economy is today, I cannot blame any young man for not wanting to take on the responsibility of a woman with a ready-made family of three or four kids, but I condemn the man who adds another lot to the litter and then leaves, blaming the cruel Sapphire for chasing him away.

The men who get involved with these young girls with babies know that the young women in their neighborhood are trapped. These men continue trying to take advantage of these young girls. Once the baby is born the guy figures he can always get his foot in the door.

Foolishly, the young girl thinks that having a baby will make the young man care for her or feel obligated to her. Somehow this young girl thinks that she will be different from the legions of other women with babies and no men. Her love will be better than the love of those other women and she will be saved. Somehow, blissfully ignorant of the limitations of the men in the pond in which she is fishing, each girl feels that she will be the lucky one to catch a good man and be saved.

I cannot totally condemn these foolish young women because I see the same willful blindness in others. The alcoholic or drug addict thinks this will be his last drink or fix; the gambler thinks this time he will score big; the Christian thinks that she will be saved where thousands (or millions) of others have perished because her prayers are better. She is special—God is with her and will protect her because she is a better Christian than the rest. This kind of thinking is endemic in our society. Few people want to acknowledge that they are just as ordinary as everyone else. Everyone wants to be special when in reality 99 percent of us are just ordinary.

The young girl who has nothing to offer but her love never stops to consider that even if the baby's father does care for her there is no magic by which the dropouts in her world can acquire a career that will suddenly allow them to support her and a family. The myth of black magic love conquering all is just that, a myth. The proponents of the strong black love myth, like the *Black Man's Guide*, fail to warn the young naive readers that success requires more hard work than it does love. The proponents of these myths fail to warn the young naive readers that personal gratification at home does not guarantee success in the marketplace.

Instead of providing these girls with silly myths that all too often work only in the middle-class white world, someone should tell these young girls that loving a man or bearing his children does not guarantee that the bacon will be brought home. Bringing home the bacon requires a skill or sweat and the good fortune to have a job or a career. A career may take ten years after high school to build, sometimes longer. For example, to become a lawyer takes nineteen years of schooling, twelve years of pre-college study, four years of undergraduate study, and three years of law school. To a seventeen-year-old black youth who does not know the meaning of delayed gratification, twelve years may as well be one hundred years, or nineteen years may as well be one thousand years. And so, the make-babies-and-run game gets played over and over again. It requires no planning, no hard work, and provides instant gratification.

Most of these men have watched some other man run the same game on their mothers and have *learned the game well.* Having "a man" in the home has not proved a workable solution for many black families since many of the black men who are in the home are part of the problem. The mere presence of a penis in the household cannot magically solve problems that are hundreds of years old. The thousands of black male youths who know the make-babies-and-run game oh so well have usually learned the game *from another black man*. To suggest that these misguided men are the solution to any black woman's problems is a crime that will no doubt ensure the black female's continued oppression. Wherever these game-playing brothers go, trouble will follow. A man who is a menace to himself and to his community cannot magically bring stability to a family.

Contrary to what many of our youth are encouraged to believe, there is no magic in having a black dick. There is, however, much magic in having self-respect and respect for others; determination, fortitude and courage; common sense and the ability to plan further ahead than the next weekend or paycheck. A man with these qualities is the kind of man that these young girls need but which their world is sorely lacking. To suggest that these young girls continue to wait for a man to help them is a travesty. Unless these young women dig their heels in and start shoveling dirt today, they will never get out of the hole they are in and their children will be buried with them, as will their grandchildren and great-grandchildren.

If we continue to assume that men's experiences are more important than women's experiences and that what is most crucial among men's experiences is their ability to assert themselves patriarchally, these girls and their families will continue to perish while they are ignored. These young girls and their children need help now, not next week, next month, next year or whenever the men in their world get their acts together. For these young girls, to wait is to die, slowly but surely.

Eventually, these young girls wake up old, disappointed and bitter, trapped in a decaying area of the city, trained to do little but watch television all day and to pray. They pray for miracles that never come. Their daily prayer is that their children or grandchildren do not get killed on the way home from school because "the neighborhood is so bad." Their numbers are legion.

The myths presented in the *Black Man's Guide* cannot help these young girls. There will never be black knights for these girls. The men in their world are as troubled as they are. Obedience and submission to the men in their world is not likely to improve their condition and will most likely result in their continued abuse. Few men who have prospects for a good future are going to weigh themselves down with the burden of a seventeen-year-old girl who already has three babies. Most of the men she meets will use her for free sex and a place to spend the night, but that is about all. If she is lucky she might get taken to the movies or the park. She is simply too big a handicap.

These young women have no future unless they make up their minds to break their own chains. To encourage them to believe in the American dream of the knight and the pedestal, or to wait for a man to give direction to their lives is slow but sure death for these young women. Each day they sink deeper and deeper into a bottomless black hole from which soon they will never be able to escape to daylight. They cling desperately to the bottom rung of the ladder of life. So much of their energy is consumed in maintaining their unstable grip that there is no energy left to even think about climbing up. Adulthood for them is a nightmare that continues even in the daylight hours.

By adulthood, whatever their circumstances and wherever they live, most black women are well acquainted with the black man's taunts of "Sapphire!" and of the "kinder, gentler white woman." At this stage, many black women whose spirits were not broken in their youth simply give up on the black male. Some devote themselves to their children with a fervor, while others return to school or devote themselves to their jobs with a passion. Others simply sign off and let life go by.

I chose to attend law school because I have not given up on the idea of justice however I can get it, while one of my very best friends chose suicide. After three failed marriages she decided that life simply was not worth it. Unfortunately, she left a black daughter behind who is struggling to this date to understand what happened to her mother. Those of us who loved her mother do not know where to begin to rectify her daughter's anger and agony. No doubt this lost and loving child will be branded as another hostile Sapphire when she matures because she has learned to challenge the world for the mistreatment of black women and to demand an explanation from those who stand silently by.

My heart bleeds for young black girls today. I for one would not want to be young again. The pain and anxiety were too great. At forty, I am happy discovering that I am a whole person with self-worth outside of the man with whom I am associated, if I choose to associate with one who is available. My entire life is no longer planned totally around someone else's needs. I have a corner for myself.

Do I think that law will save me or give me justice? Not always, but the scars inflicted in the courtroom heal much quicker than the scars inflicted in the bedroom. In the courtroom, one's guard is always up, not like the relaxed state into which one frequently lapses in the home or community in which one supposedly belongs or is loved. There is no love in the courtroom and everyone knows it. There is only a fight to the finish in which both parties try to come out on top, but even the bullies must wait their turn to speak. There are rules and a referee to make sure that the foul play does not get out of hand.

However, the battle in the courtroom is a much fairer fight than the battle in the bedroom. The loser in the courtroom battle is seldom carried away on a stretcher, and can always appeal. My grandmother and aunt, like many black women in America, did not live to fight another day. The rules in their game were much harsher. Their deaths were final and there was no appeal. I hope to fight many battles before I die. Therefore I choose to fight in the courtroom.

Chapter 4

The Myth of Matriarchy

The term matriarch implies the existence of a social order in which women have social and political power.[26] Such condition in no way resembles the social status of black women in American society. The sociologists who labeled black women "matriarchs" conveniently never discussed the social status customarily accorded a woman under a matriarchy, because clearly the black woman has never experienced this status. No matriarchy has ever existed in America, in spite of the *Moynihan Report's* proclamation "that the Negro community has been forced into a matriarchal structure which because it is so out of line with the rest of American society, seriously retards the progress of the group as a whole...."[27]

Interestingly, as long as black women were working as agricultural sharecroppers and domestic servants or in low-wage service jobs, white males evinced no concern about the dangerous black matriarchy. However, in the years after World War II when black females began to break into the industrial arena and to garner decent clerical jobs in the government sector that had the potential to lead to the black females' independence of male domination, white males became strangely concerned about the black "matriarchy," even though some poor and widowed white women performed the same dual role.

I cannot help suspecting that the white male's concern over the so-called black matriarchy and the touted emasculation of the black male was a facade for the white man's real concern—ensuring the continued domination of white women. The independence of any woman in a male-dominated society is dangerous in that other women might decide that independence might not be a bad thing for them either. The *Moynihan Report*, which was the source of the matriarchy theory (and which was also pretty racist with its subjective pronouncements of the "tangle of pathology" of the "Negro" disguised as objective reasoning) served as an implicit warning to white women (or more particularly to white men) that if white women persisted in entering the work force in large numbers as black women had done, and demanded equal pay for comparable work and related benefits in order to secure financial independence, they too would endanger the basic family structural unit as defined by society—the nuclear family under male protection (domination).[28]

What is also particularly interesting about the *Moynihan Report* is that those black men who quickly embraced its matriarchy theory failed to adopt its solution. Moynihan's solution to restore the black male's lost or stolen pride was to place large numbers of black men in the ultimate male sphere, the military, where they would be safe from the meddling matriarch. However, Moynihan failed to make a prediction as to when Congress or the President might declare another war and what the chances were that all the newly cured black brothers would be killed in that war.

Labeling the black woman a matriarch was a direct contradiction to the accurate portrayal of the black woman's experience in America. A matrilineal line of descent may have been legally imposed on the slave community, but this was done to ensure the slave status of offspring born of slave mothers and white fathers. Thus matriliny in the slave class was not a function of matriarchal dominance but instead was a function of institutional rape.[29] Rather bizarrely, in the *Moynihan Report* we are told that the matriliny of the slave class has produced female dominance.

At the very time white sociologists proclaimed the existence of the matriarchal order in the black family structure, black women represented one of the largest socially and economically deprived groups in America. The so-called black matriarch is a kind of folk character, much like the loyal and docile Aunt Jemima, fashioned by whites out of half-truths and lies about the involuntary condition of black women in America. The misuse of the term "matriarch" has led many unknowing people to identify any black woman present in a household where no male resides as a matriarch. Nothing could be further from the truth.

Within past matriarchal societies the woman was almost always economically secure. The matriarch was usually the owner of property. In a matriarchy, the female typically had complete control over her body. Female children were preferred in a matriarchy because they continue the family which boys cannot. Domestic work was considered degrading to the woman in a matriarchy just as it is considered beneath the male's dignity in a male-dominated society. This clearly is not the situation in the black female-headed households in America, and yet many Americans ignorantly continue to label the single, black, female head of household a matriarch. Perhaps this is not surprising in a country in which the poorest downtrodden man in America, even one living on a New York City sidewalk in a cardboard box over a warm vent, will proudly claim to be "king" of his castle. Americans have never been fond of reality.

The same ignorance that allows a belief in matriarchy allows supporters of the matriarchy theory to assume that the jobs black women were able to acquire enabled them to elevate their status above the black male's when in actuality most of the jobs acquired by black women were low level service and agricultural jobs. On the average, black men have always made more money than black women and historically have made more than white females.[30] (*see appendix A*)

Historically, the number of black female employees in the job market has leveled off at around 40 percent. Only recently has the number of white women entering the market approached this level. It will be interesting to see if the continued entry of large numbers of highly educated white females into the marketplace results in the black male's being booted from his second-place wage-earning status (behind the white male) to third place (in front of the black woman, who has always been in fourth place). Since white females, like black females, are generally more educated than black males, logically white females should come to earn more than black males, too. At least educational qualifications are part of the reasoning that is used to predict that black women will eventually come to out-earn black males in the market. The other part is that white men feel less threatened by black women. Will not these same white men feel even less threatened by their white mothers, wives, sisters and lovers?

Why is there such a stink about the predictions that black females will eventually come to out-earn black males, but no concern that white females will eventually come to outearn black males? Is one scenario more acceptable than the other? No doubt there is an explanation for this double standard, though what I cannot imagine. Strangely, the black men who express outrage at the prospect that black women may soon come to out-earn them seem unconcerned that the average white woman may also soon come to out-earn the average black male.

It will also be interesting to see if the black mates of the white females who come to out-earn them in the market will feel emasculated by their wives' higher earning power, assuming these black men's white wives work. Most interesting of all will be the reaction of the black men who are bumped by white females in the market, but who nonetheless must support their white stay-at-home wives. Will these black men become resentful of white women as much as they are resentful of black women? Will these black men go home to their white wives and complain about the white bitches at work? Will the black community express outrage if these black men should experience difficulty in supporting their white wives? Will white women be asked to step aside so that black men with white wives will have a better shot at advancing on the job? It will truly be interesting to see if black men make half the demands of white women that they have made of black women.

From the black males' total focus on black women out-earning them in the market, one could conclude that somehow it is more odious to be out-earned by a black female than to be out-earned by a white female. Is being bumped or out-earned in the market by a white woman more palatable to the black man than being out-earned by a black woman in that same market? Why is this very likely scenario never discussed? Why is scorn heaped upon the black female for any perceived benefit she reaps in the market, but no scorn heaped upon the white woman in that same market? Why the double standard? No doubt some will offer the possibility of a negative shift in the black man's position in the job market as a good reason to keep all women out of the labor market, except those women who are needed to do the menial tasks beneath a man's dignity, or the tasks for which we all know that women are more qualified, i.e., the jobs that have the lowest wages (waitressing, teaching, nursing, secretarial work).

If women are ever granted equal opportunity in the job market, every woman in that market with more education than the black man will out-earn the black man! This means not only black women, but also white women, Asian women, Latinas, etc. Those black men in the market who are concerned about their egos being crushed by the black female dominance in the market should be far more concerned about the prospect of being out-earned by non-black females than by black females because there are ten times as many non-black females as there are black females! At least the black women are likely to bring some of their money back to the black community, the very black community that is so critical of them. Not many of the white women who out-earn black men are going to bring one cent of their money to the black community.

Instead of bitching about Sapphire, black men should be beating a path to the black community and helping the brothers there get an education so they can at least try to make a dent in the marketplace. Are black men so blinded by hatred for Sapphire that they cannot see that if the day ever comes that Sapphire out-earns the brothers, it will only be because *every other woman in the market also out-earns the brothers!* Sapphire is always in last place in the hierarchy of women. This will never change in white America. Are our memories that short?

If the black community does not get more educated black men into the market before male dominance comes to an end, which like it or not is rapidly approaching, Sapphire will be the least of the black man's problems. She will be just a small part of the thousands of women who are more educated than black men and who will therefore out-earn black men. We are only wasting valuable time trying to crucify Sapphire. She is not the problem. Even if she out-earns the brothers, she is not likely to discriminate against black men merely because of skin color. Like the white male scholars who initially examined the black family and developed the matriarchy theory, our focus is skewed.

White male scholars who first examined the black family, examined it in the context of attempting to discover the ways in which the black family unit resembled the white family unit. These men were biased by their personal prejudices against women assuming an active role in family decision-making; thus they labeled black women, who had no choice but to make these decisions, "matriarchs." Most of these white males were educated in elite white institutions that often excluded both women and blacks. Even when blacks and women were admitted to these institutions, the dominant white male view prevailed. Thus the independence, willpower, and initiative of black women was seen as an attack on the masculinity of black men, much as such behavior on the part of white women would have been seen as an attack on the masculinity of white men. These men argued that the black woman's active role as a mother and bread-winner deprived black men of their patriarchal status in the home, when in reality the black man was stripped of that status with the docking of the first slave ship hundreds of years ago. The emancipation did not revive that status.

Patriarchal status is generally conferred on the man who is the sole economic "provider" for his family. Of course, "provider" is a loaded word. It generally assumes a solid middle-class existence. Thus even if their black wives did not work, many black men still would not be considered "providers" because of their low wages, and thus not true patriarchs. Ironically, the argument that black female matriarchs were responsible for stripping the black male of his patriarchal status was readily accepted by black males even though it was an image created by white males. Both "patriarchy" and "matriarchy" are value-laden buzzwords that are used to evoke predictable responses in the white community. However, both words are of dubious meaning in relation to the black community and should therefore be viewed with suspicion. In spite of the black male's willingness to embrace patriarchy, true patriarchy remains an elusive dream for the average black male as true matriarchy for the black female.

The independent role black women were forced to play in both the labor market and in the family unit was automatically perceived as unfeminine. Negative attitudes toward working women have always existed in America. Just as white men were socialized to regard the entry of white women into the labor market as a threat to male positions and masculinity, black men have been socialized to regard the entry of black women into the labor market with similar suspicions. The matriarchy theory provided a convenient framework within which to condemn the working black woman for problems that she did not create. Black men were thereby able to add the matriarchy myth to their arsenal of psychological weapons (most notable of which is the Bible) to demand that black women assume a more passive and subservient role in the home.

The black man is not alone in this negative response to women in the labor market. Most men in a patriarchal society fear and resent women who do not assume the traditional passive, non-assertive role. It was truly unfortunate that black men failed to see that by shifting the responsibility for the unemployment of black men onto black women, white males who had routinely and deliberately oppressed blacks were able to establish a bond of solidarity with black men based on their mutual sexist ideology. Thus the black female was the enemy instead of the white male. Just as whites used the myth that all black women were loose or immoral to devalue black womanhood, they used the matriarchy myth to impress upon the consciousness of all America that black women were masculinized, castrating bitches, somehow not real women.

A similar rationale had been used during slavery to explain the black woman's ability to survive without the direct aid of a male and her ability to perform tasks that were culturally defined as "masculine." White males hypothesized that black slave women were not "real" women but instead some kind of masculinized sub-human creatures. Sojourner Truth, who had been a slave the first forty years of her life and who had watched most of her five children sold into slavery, bared her breasts before an assembly of whites at an anti-slavery rally in Indiana to prove that she was indeed a woman. To whites, it was incomprehensible that a woman could have survived such a harsh existence.

The black female slave's ability to perform "masculine" tasks and to endure hardship, pain and deprivation while still performing womanly tasks threatened patriarchal myths about the nature of women's inherent physiological difference and inferiority. Ironically, by forcing black female slaves to perform the same work that black male slaves performed, white male patriarchs unwittingly contradicted their own sexist ideology that women were inferior because they lacked physical prowess. No "lady" was supposed to be able to endure the hardships imposed on black women during slavery, but the black woman did. Unfortunately, the black woman is still paying the price for her strong desire and ability to survive under extremely trying conditions.

That the Sapphire identity is projected onto any black woman who dares to openly express anger, bitterness, or rage about her lot is not surprising since Christian mythology depicts woman as the source of all sin and evil. Racist mythology combined with this sexist mythology simply designates the black woman as the epitome of womanly evil and sinfulness.[31] The progression is logical however irrational. What is surprising is that many black men so readily buy into the myth of the evil black female, after having been victims of the system themselves.

This is not to say that some black women have not bought into the patriarchy theory as well.[32] Unlike many of the white men who responded to the materialistic demands of their wives by becoming devotees of the discipline of work, some black men have reacted to their wives' demands with hostility. Thus we hear constant complaints about the materialistic Sapphire. However, some black men who realize the difficulty of making ends meet with one paycheck are more supportive and accepting of their wives being in the labor force than white men.[33] On occasion it has been the black woman who has been the most incensed at the black man's not assuming the role as sole provider for the family. The following extraction from an essay by Gail Stokes entitled *Black Woman to Black Man* accurately expresses the rage of some working black women who have equated manhood with the ability of their husbands to be the sole economic provider in the family and who feel cheated when black men refuse to accept the role:

> Of course you will say, "How can I love you and want to be with you when I come home and you're looking like a slob? Why white women never open the door for their husbands the way you black bitches do."
> I should guess not, you ignorant man. Why should they be in such a state when they've got maids like me to do everything for them? There is no screaming at the kids for her, no standing over the hot stove; everything is done for her, and whether her man loves her or not, he provides... provides... do you hear that, nigger? PROVIDES![34]

One could easily conclude that such expressed frustrations assume that the black male who is not the sole provider for his family is selfish, lazy, and irresponsible. However, even this contempt for the black man's failure to provide is not necessarily an expression of the repudiation of male dominance. It could well be an acknowledgement of the wholehearted embrace of the ideal of patriarchy and an expression of disappointment at the black man's failure to accept his responsibility under the system of patriarchy.

I shall never forget how stunned I was, in the years that I worked the electrical trade, to discover how many of the white men I worked with, men that even many whites would call red-necks, sent their wives and children on luxury vacations while themselves staying on the job in order to work and to pay for the vacations. Some black men would have called these white men fools. In spite of the racism and sexism of some who proudly expressed their allegiance to rednecks, white socks, and Blue-Ribbon beer, I could not help admiring their willingness to make economic sacrifices for their families, even those who openly discussed both the wife and the girlfriend(s).

Because I was *persona non grata* in my own local union and would eternally be last hired, first fired, I frequently worked on the road as an electrician in a local other than my own. When I was on the road, I once saw a white man cry because his ex-wife constantly called the job claiming she needed extra money for the kids when he knew, and all his friends on the job knew, that half of the money he was sending his wife was being given to another man who was too lazy to work. This man's friends told him he was crazy, but he was not willing to take the chance that his children might be deprived by their mother's foolishness. Those who openly berated him, silently loaned him money whenever he ran short, which was often even though we were making well over $20 per-hour and frequently worked seven days a week. At age thirty-five, all that he owned, except his pickup truck, would fit into one suitcase. He was the personification of the provider that many women hope to find, but few do find. It is understandable that those women who buy into the myth of the male provider are bitterly disappointed when their men are unable to provide. Subsequent disillusionment is an unfortunate draw-back to the promotion of myths. One may well be left bitter and angry.

Many black women, like many black men and white women, express great hostility toward the white male power structure because they are eager to gain access to that power. Their expressions of anger are often less a critique of the social order than a reaction to the fact that they have not been allowed full participation in the power game.[35] The black woman who takes such a position and is willing to trade sub-mission for protection could well be angry when she does not get the benefit of the bargain, protection and support. The black male who takes such a position may well hope to gain public recognition of his manhood by seeking to demonstrate that he is the dominant figure in the black family and thereby demand the submission of the black female. The white woman who takes such a position may well be as oppressive of minorities as the white male has been, or more so since she has to prove herself in order to be initiated into the club into which most white men are born.

The result of former outsiders gaining access to the white male power structure could well be the continued oppression of those in a dis-advantaged position, thus the need to implement a more humane sys-tem for the distribution of goods and services, as opposed to continuing one that has worked well for dominant white males, but only for domi-nant white males. The struggle of blacks against racial imperialism has taught us that wherever there exists a master-slave relationship or an oppressor-oppressed relationship, violence and hatred permeate all aspects of life.[36] The mounting hatred and violence in black male-female relationships is directly correlated to the dynamics of oppression.

It would be unfortunate indeed if our romanticized notions of the nobility of our blackness and our differentness from whites, i.e., the myth of the noble savage, caused us to fail to see the parallel between the decaying patriarchal social order in the white community, and the black community's insistence that black women also be willing to exchange submission for protection. All of the problems between the black male and black female have not been caused by racism. Many of the problems have been caused by sexism, and continue to be caused by sexism. Sweeping the problem under the rug will not make it go away. Sexism, like racism, fosters and perpetuates violence and hatred between men and women be they black or white.

It is regrettable but understandable that some black women have embraced the matriarchy theory. For some black women the matriarchy theory represented society's first recognition of the black woman's struggle to provide for and to contribute to the black family. Compared to the usual taunts of Sapphire, niggah bitch, and "hoe", to be called "matriarch" was a relief. The delusion that black women exercised meaningful social and political control over their lives provided a much needed boost to an often otherwise solitary and weary existence. However, the false sense of power black women are thereby encouraged to feel decreases the likelihood that black women will organize collectively to fight against oppression.

If black women are lulled into complacency by this false sense of being a powerful matriarch, both white men and black men benefit. Even if white males should have to give up their domination of black males, the coalition formed between black males and white males would enable all males to dominate all females. Last place will be reserved for the black female, behind the kind and gentle white woman. Ironically, it is black women who are most often victimized by the very sexism we refuse to acknowledge as a force of oppression.

The point is not that Sapphire should rise up and do battle with the brothers, but that black women should stop trying (or being forced) to be martyrs and acknowledge that we are human beings with feelings like everyone else. We too have needs that can no longer be put aside. We are tired of having to be both mothers and fathers to our children but are not about to abdicate our roles as caring human beings for mere economic support. We have contributed much to this world and therefore have much to say about its future, our future, and the future of our children. We are not interested in merely replicating the white social order in black face. We are truly concerned with liberty and justice for all, the promise that was held out by the founding fathers but never fulfilled. We do not want our freedom at the price of someone else's liberty. Our world view is true equality for all, not the shortsighted goal of submission for protection. It has not worked for the white man and white woman and will not work for us. The group of elite white females who have been the most protected for centuries have taken to the streets to break the chains of their "protection."

Many black women want equality, not protection! We gladly continue to accept responsibility for the world around us! We have learned well that as long as any of us is oppressed all of us are oppressed. We are tired of oppression.

Unquestioned obedience is a fool's paradise that allows human greed and ego to run amok. This was true in the days of slavery when white men reigned unquestioned, and is still true today, even though many in the black community now propose that black men should now be allowed to reign unquestioned. Has slavery not taught us the dangers of allowing men to reign unquestioned? Are black men and black women so blind to our history that we are strangers living in the same land doomed to repeating white history in black face? Are we to go our separate ways after coming this far? What sorrow, the price of companionship—submission for protection—that is too high.

Chapter 5

The Problem of Perspective

Suppose for a moment, that a teacher instructs two students to sort a box of randomly colored, sized and numbered blocks into appropriate piles. The students are likely to sort the blocks into similar piles. However, if one of the students is color-blind, she will sort the blocks quite differently. Which sorting method will be deemed most appropriate will in large part turn on whether or not the teacher is also color-blind. Most significantly, if the instructor teaching the class is color-blind, the student who sees the added dimension of color will experience constant frustration. This is the daily frustration felt by blacks and women who are the victims of discrimination on the basis of race and sex.

Sex discrimination, like the concept of race discrimination, may be approached from either the perspective of the victim or the perspective of the perpetrator.[37] From the victim's perspective, both race and sex discrimination describe those conditions of actual existence as a member of the class discriminated against. The victim's perspective includes both the objective conditions of life and the consciousness associated with those objective conditions. For example, the victims of both race and sex discrimination perceive that his or her lack of jobs, money, education and housing (the objective conditions) is associated with society's perception of him or her as a member of a group rather than as an individual (the consciousness associated with those objective conditions).

The perpetrator, however, sees race and sex discrimination not as conditions, but as a series of acts inflicted on the victim by the perpetrator. The perpetrator focuses on what particular perpetrators have done to the victims rather than on the overall life situation of the victim class. Thus despite years of oppression leaving their mark in the form of identifiable consequences of racism and sexism, such as "residential segregation, inadequate education, overrepresentation in lowest-status jobs, disproportionately low political power, and a disproportionate share of the least and worst of everything valued most in our materialistic society,"[38] society is unwilling to look at the conditions under which blacks live, or the conditions under which women live and conclude that something must be done about discrimination, unless the victim can point the finger at a particular individual who is responsible for the particular condition. This myopic insistence that "the innocence of whites weighs more heavily than [both] the past wrongs committed upon blacks [and women] and the benefits that whites [and men] derived from those wrongs"[39] is why sex discrimination, like race discrimination, is virtually impossible to prove or eradicate.

Surprisingly, many black men who have suffered as victims of race discrimination are unable to see the sex discrimination women complain about because as perpetrators of that sex discrimination, they can only view sex discrimination from the perpetrator perspective—as a series of acts inflicted on the victim by the perpetrator, whereas they may clearly be able to view race discrimination from their perspective as victims—as the objective conditions of life and the consciousness associated with those objective conditions. Thus clearly the problem in seeking to remedy race and sex discrimination is one of the perspective from which we interpret the law or reality. "[S]pecific interpretations proceed largely from the world view of the interpreter."[40]

The victim perspective of race and sex discrimination suggests that the problem will not be solved until the conditions associated with the discrimination have been eliminated. From this perspective, to remedy the conditions of race and sex discrimination would demand affirmative efforts to change the condition. From the perpetrator's perspective, however, the remedial task is merely to neutralize the inappropriate conduct of the perpetrator. Thus just as the Supreme Court would have us believe that ours is a color-blind society and that racial discrimination is best remedied by removing the few who inappropriately act as racists rather than seeking to remedy the conditions under which blacks suffer, black males would have black females believe that the conditions to which black females are subject in the black community (assault, abandonment, rape, murder, and other daily indignities) are the result of a few misguided brothers who have not learned how to respect their women, and that sex discrimination does not exist in the black community (even though we all know it exists in the white community). In the alternative, some black males would have black females believe that all conditions that negatively impact black females in the black community are the white man's fault.

The perpetrator perspective assumes that the world is composed of isolated individuals whose actions are unrelated to and separate from the social fabric and without historical continuity. Thus, we may speak of a few racist white men or a few misguided brothers as the problem. From the perpetrator perspective, race and sex discrimination are not social phenomenon, but rather the misguided acts of a few individuals. The perpetrator perspective assumes that but for the conduct of the misguided ones, the system of equality would work to provide a distribution of goods and services without racial and sexual disparities. Therefore where deprivations exist that do correlate with race or sex, those deprived would be deserving of deprivation because of insufficient merit on their individual parts. Thus, when a black man with credentials similar to those of his white counterpart cannot find a job, it is because something about him is unmeritorious. Or when a black woman is beaten senseless or abandoned by her black husband, she must have done something to deserve it. Some with the perpetrator perspective would even extend this logic to rape, (i.e., the woman must have done something to deserve it.) This system produces a world where vested rights (seniority) or natural rights (the Bible says that man should dominate woman) and objective selection systems (the "most qualified" prevails), all of which serve to prevent victims from experiencing any change in their social and economic conditions, have nothing to do with the problem of race or sex discrimination.

Central to the perpetrator perspective are the notions of fault and causation.[41] The fault idea is manifested in the assertion that only intentional discrimination is bad. Thus if all the black females on stage, screen and the covers of popular magazines accidentally happen to be light-skinned but no one intended to discriminate against dark-skinned females, there is no discrimination. Likewise, if a company historically has hired blacks only as janitors and low-wage clerical workers, there is no discrimination as long as the company did not intend to discriminate. Of course we may determine the employer's intent only by asking him, but he is an honorable white man and will always tell the truth, as those native American Indians lucky enough to survive the first onslaught of the white man in America will verify. As long as the perpetrator did not intend to discriminate, it is the victim's tough luck if he or she continually receives the short end of the stick.

From the perpetrator perspective, the perpetrator need not feel any personal responsibility for the conditions associated with the discrimination and is justified in becoming righteously indignant if expected to bear any burdens connected with remedying the unfortunate situation. Thus just as those who have reaped the benefits of the public economy and the institutions that arose from the profitable slave trade and the institution of slavery may express righteous indignation at being asked to give something in return for the benefits reaped, the black male may express his horror at being confronted with the rape of black women. It is certainly not his fault that the white man's laws granted any man the license to rape a black woman and that the effects linger today. Why should black men be burdened with trying to turn back the tide? Likewise, why should black men concern themselves with wage discrimination against women? Black men did not make the rules. The white man did!

The causation requirement (the second central notion of the perpetrator perspective) serves to distinguish the conditions that a victim perceives to be associated with discrimination with those that society will acknowledge. For example, it is common knowledge that blacks experience more difficulty in finding housing accommodations than any group in America. The "tipping point" phenomenon is not a figment of the black imagination. Most whites will not live where they fear they will not remain the dominant majority. Studies of housing patterns have shown that when the black population in an area approaches 20 percent, white flight becomes the order of the day.[42] Society has been willing to acknowledge that this obvious public discrimination should be eliminated. However, society refuses to acknowledge that discrimination by private individuals should also be eliminated. Though it seems perfectly obvious that private discrimination is at the root of public discrimination, how could one ever prove this in a court of law? Because the victim cannot prove it, society does not have to acknowledge it. Thus, discrimination by individuals in the private sphere, by private clubs, by religious organizations and by landlords that own less than three dwelling units is perfectly legal.

Even in the realm of recognized public discrimination, the burden falls on the victim to prove causation. The victim must isolate the particular condition of discrimination and link this condition to the behavior of an identified blameworthy perpetrator. If the victim cannot prove that a particular act caused a particular problem, society need not acknowledge the discrimination, whether large numbers of victims continue to suffer or not.

Under the current state of the law, black victims readily understand that racial discrimination will never be eliminated since the real intent is not to alleviate the conditions in the black community, but merely to placate the perpetrator class by punishing the errant few racists that are stupid enough to get caught red-handed. The result is that the Bull Connors of the world no longer shout from the roof tops that no niggers are allowed, but strangely enough, the black face remains absent in large segments of America. As long as the perpetrator view prevails, which no doubt it will as long as the perpetrator remains in power, the masses of blacks will never get justice in the civil rights arena.

Ironically, many black men view sex discrimination with the same thick-headed arrogance with which the dominant white class views racial discrimination. They argue that sex discrimination in the black community is non-existent because unlike white men, black men have never intended to discriminate against black women and there has been no proof that any particular condition of black women has been caused by an identifiable group of black men. That the condition of black women continues to deteriorate is ignored.

In spite of her touted strength, the black woman is at the bottom rung of the ladder of life in America. She makes less money and is subject to as much or more brutality than any other defined group. As the condition of blacks in general has not improved where the remedy has been limited to one black face at a time, the condition of black women in America is not likely to change soon if their remedy is limited to one woman at a time. There are simply too many black women who need help.

Black men, like white men, deny their common historical and cultural heritage in which sexism has, and still does play a dominant role. Because of this shared experience, black men and white men inevitably share many ideas, attitudes and beliefs that attach significance to an individual's sex and induce negative feelings and opinions about women. Just as blacks are viewed as somehow less worthy than whites, women are viewed as somehow less worthy than men, and black women are viewed the least worthy of all. To the extent that this cultural belief system has influenced both white men and black men, both are oppressors of women. Both fail to recognize the ways in which their cultural experience has influenced their beliefs about the feminine gender or the occasions on which those beliefs affect their actions. A large part of the behavior that produces sex discrimination is influenced by unconscious motivations.[43] Thus the behavior is hard to redress.

This is in part because the human mind defends itself against the discomfort of guilt by denying or refusing to recognize those ideas and beliefs that conflict with what the individual has learned is honorable or right. While our historical experience has made both racism and sexism an integral part of our culture, society has more recently idealistically rejected racism and sexism as immoral. Therefore when an individual experiences conflict between racist or sexist ideas and the new societal ethic that condemns those ideas, the mind attempts to exclude the racism or sexism from consciousness.

Additionally, our culture transmits certain beliefs and preferences. Because these beliefs are so much a part of the culture, they are not experienced as lessons on a conscious level. Instead, they are experienced as part of the individual's rational scheme of perceptions of the world. Because racism and sexism are so deeply ingrained in our culture, it is generally transmitted by tacit understanding. Thus, even if a child is not told that blacks or women are inferior, the child learns that lesson by observing the behavior of others. Because the lesson has not been articulated, it is not experienced at a conscious level.

I did not have to be explicitly told that black women were less worthy than white men or white women or black men. The message was fed to me subconsciously in every direction in which I turned. My father viewed women as less worthy and my mother accepted her lot; the church viewed women as less worthy and the women there accepted their lot; the law and court system viewed women as less worthy and the women there had no choice but to accept their lot; both the black community and the white community viewed women as less worthy. Compounded with the fact that I was black and viewed as less worthy on that account, I learned early in life that I was the lowest of the low. The only place where I had refuge was school.

As long as I maintained an "A" average, the teachers thought I was important and the students did not bother me except when they wanted help with their homework. I never had a single fight, except my first week of school in the first grade when some boys picked on me, and my older sister beat them up. Never dreaming that I was being taken advantage of, I was happy when the teachers let me stay in at recess or after school to grade the other students' papers or asked me to go to the library to do research for them. It did not matter whether I was black or ugly or poor. Even the so-called mean white teachers were nice to me, if only because they thought I was a good student. In my heart I knew I was just another nigger, but at school, I could escape for a while. Sometimes my teachers even asked me what I thought instead of telling me what I should think.

I was happier at school than I was anywhere else, because at school I was not relegated to a "place," at least not until I went to college and entered a non-traditional field. Until I graduated from high school, school was the only place where I ever felt free. At school I could breathe, and I thrived there.

I have learned much in school, though not always the lessons I was supposed to learn and not always from the teachers. Some of the most interesting lessons in school have been those outside the textbooks. One lesson I inadvertently learned in a law school classroom brought home the impossibility of solving problems of sex and race discrimination to me.

Last year, I enrolled in a Civil Rights class taught by a young, brilliant, extremely attractive, black female law professor. She was clearly an enigma to many white students in the class, but her Harvard credentials satisfied most that she was at least qualified. Sometimes I would sit in class, watching the students and laughing to myself at how her mere appearance seemed to baffle the class. Many just could not understand how this young black woman who could easily pass for a fashion model could know more than they knew and worst of all, tie even the most articulate speaker into knots. She was a bitter pill for many in the class. On occasion, some white students could be seen staring with their mouths open. Although this very brilliant professor was younger than I, it was a pleasure to be taught by a "young upstart." I loved to watch and listen to her teach. In addition to having smarts, she had wisdom. There was always a waiting list for her class.

On the first day, she warned the class that her class would be different from the usual law school classes in that students would be encouraged to relate real life experience to the course materials. Customarily, after the first year of law school, many law students sign off from the inhuman process of grueling work. To those who sign off, anything except that which will be covered on the final exam is considered a waste of time. But this class was different. The tensions ran so high that frequently there were tears, harsh words, and continued debates in the hallway. This class was the highlight of my law school career.

The week we discussed race-hate speech was illustrative of the double bind racial minorities experience in law school and in life, and also illustrative of the impossibility of the eradication of discrimination. The analogy of this double bind is easily translated to black women. For a week the class consensus seemed to be that because of the high value our society places on free speech and the expression of political ideas, those who were subjected to abusive speech would have to endure it as the price of being a member of society. The remedy for hate speech was thought to be more speech.

Then one day there was an outburst in which a black female student characterized something a white male student said as "bullshit." The tide turned! Suddenly there was silence and hostility from the white students. The tension was still so great a couple of days later that the professor stopped the class to ask what the problem was. The same students who had championed the value of free speech and the marketplace of ideas in situations where the vilest of invectives were hurled at minorities complained bitterly that their speech had been chilled because of one student's indiscriminate use of the word "bullshit."

What was most disturbing about the whole incident was that most of the traditional white students in the class, who had sat through almost the entire semester of Civil Rights and who professed to "understand" racial politics, could not see the parallel between the intimidation they felt in the classroom that day when their basic notions about their value system and self-worth were challenged and the intimidation blacks experience everyday in life when, in the name of free speech, even the most malevolent of whites are given free reign to verbally abuse blacks and challenge our very right to exist. On the one hand, in our hypotheticals, class discussions and case materials, the speech of minorities was thought not to be chilled by the vilest of invectives, but on the other hand, upper-class white students were offended and felt that their speech was chilled by a single outburst from a five-foot two-inch, ninety-five-pound black female and her use of one word that could hardly be characterized as a racial epithet or slur and which was not unknown to the law school classrooms. Most white students could not see the double standard or the hypocrisy of that double standard. After almost an entire semester of lectures by a brilliant and able professor who could hold her own in any academic circle in America, racism remained a mere academic experience to the many gifted white students in the class. They simply did not get it. They could not understand what the average black child comes to understand before entering the first grade. How can this be?

When a black student in the class asked how the First Amendment (free speech) was supposed to work in the real world when it did not seem to work in a class of supposedly intelligent individuals, a white male student insisted that the classroom was different because students do not expect to feel targeted there. (Is this to say that blacks by now should have come to expect racial epithets in the world outside the classroom and thus not be upset by them?) This student clearly had experienced his legal education differently from the many non-white students who felt targeted in the classroom every day.

That same semester when a white male professor had written, "Fuck the niggers!" on the blackboard to illustrate the principles of free speech, the same white students who felt intimidated by the use of the word "bullshit" had announced that they could not understand why black students were upset by the white professor's use of a racial slur in the classroom since the slur was only intended for educational purposes. Interestingly, the white student who complained that the classroom was different from the real world as far as free speech was concerned, did not mention that part of his discomfort may have been due to the fact that the person in authority, the professor, was a black woman as was the student who made the "chilling" comment. The Civil Rights class was the complete flip side of the white students' traditional experience where the professor is white and white students are free to make all kinds of remarks and assumptions about blacks while black students sit uncomfortably at the edge of their seats. No doubt the complaining student's inability to "relate" to the authority figure was part of his discomfort. The discomfort minorities experience in law school, however, is not always limited to blacks.

In a Constitutional Law class of which I had the misfortune to be a member, a white female student once stated that the United States had no choice except to place the Japanese American citizens in prisoner of war camps during World War II. Other white students in the class quickly rallied to her defense. Needless to say the Japanese students in the class were outraged and extremely uncomfortable, as were the Korean and Chinese students because of the popular perception that they all look alike. A few Asian students rose valiantly to express their outrage and the class was stung to silence.

72

Then, as every minority student in the class expected, a few white students had the gall to explain that the white woman who unwittingly expressed her racists sentiments did not really mean what she had just said. They were quick to re-interpret the unwitting white student's comment, lest we have to admit that racism still existed, even against the "model minority." Those who were anxious to believe that racism no longer existed quickly accepted the re-interpretation of the original statement, as if they had been deaf when the initial statement was made. I never enjoyed the Constitutional Law class after that and signed off the balance of the semester.

In light of the Constitutional Law debacle, I should not have been surprised at the comments that were made in the Civil Rights class, but I was. I was surprised that even after a semester of intensive discussion about the problems of racism, many obviously bright white law students had come to understand little about the pervasive problem of racism in America. They could not see that they were just as big a part of the problem as the few bad eggs that we scapegoat for the survival of racism.

When one of the most vociferous white students in the Civil Rights class was asked which was more threatening: (1) for a white student to feel targeted when in a classroom of students where 95 percent of the students were white and where the student knows he or she is safe, or (2) for a black person walking down the street all alone at 10 o'clock at night to be confronted by a car full of white males shouting racial epithets and hurling invectives or other projectiles (like the cases we had discussed the week before when almost every white student in the class insisted that there must be freedom of speech at all costs), the protesting student could not find words to answer. No doubt he realized the hypocrisy of the double standard he had unthinkingly advocated. From the contorted look on his face one could sense that for the first time in his law school career he sensed some of the anguish minorities feel every day, or at least that free speech does not always lead to more free speech. For some, speech can be strangely silencing.

Many whites never have this experience because their view generally prevails wherever they go. Few whites are ever the lone small voice in a situation in which their self-esteem and core values of human worth are on the line. Minorities are put in this position seven days a week. As the dominant group, whites are seldom forced to step outside themselves and view the world from someone else's perspective. The only perspective they recognize and acknowledge is their own, the perpetrator perspective. This is also true of most males and their perspective of women.

Many black men occupy the perpetrator position in relation to black women. Because black males are in the dominant position, they may never have occasion to step outside themselves and consider the non-dominant black female position. Thus the black male who is outraged by his mistreatment at the hands of whites, has no idea of what the black female is complaining about when she is outraged by her treatment at the hands of black men. Sex discrimination thereby becomes as invisible and as impossible to eradicate as race discrimination. Until a problem is acknowledged, it can never be corrected.

It is very easy, but mistaken, for black men to look at the 2 or 3 percent of black women who appear to be able to deal with the most disparate of treatment and come through unscathed and conclude that there is no sex discrimination against black women—just as it is very easy, but mistaken, for whites to look at the small number of elite black males who appear to be able to deal with the most disparate of treatment and come through unscathed and conclude that there is no race discrimination. Such is not the case. The 2 or 3 percent pay a dear price that often they are not free to express. Even if the 2 or 3 percent escape unscathed by race and sex discrimination, what about the reality of the other 98 percent? Because of sheer numbers, the 2 or 3 percent can never save the 98 percent, but the 98 percent potentially can save the 2 or 3 percent. Should not our focus be on the 98 percent when they have the potential to save us all? As those who are victims of discrimination well know, our problem will not be solved until the conditions associated with the discrimination have been eliminated. Redressing individual grievances will not help the masses who continue to suffer.

Remedying the condition of the masses requires affirmative efforts to change conditions, not to provide individual remedies. Thus those women whose concerns extend no further than catching a man so that they may improve their own individual lots are shortsighted indeed. When their daughters, and granddaughters and great-granddaughters are grown, they will face the same predicament. Who will be there to help them? The solution is not to catch a man, but instead, to improve the lot of women.

When I lived in New York City, I was dismayed by the large numbers of homeless black women that I saw on the streets every day. I could not believe that no one cared about these women. Some were as young as fourteen, others were as old as sixty-five. The sorriest sight I ever saw was that of a fifty-five-year-old black woman walking in the snow wearing thong sandals, holding her dress out from her leg because there was no skin on her leg. If she had let go of the dress, it would have stuck to her leg, which was an ulcerated mass of raw flesh. I stopped a policeman and asked if he could help her. He just shook his head and walked away from me. I was sick to my stomach. She was one of thousands of hopeless cases.

When it rained, these poor women walked around wearing plastic garbage bags because they did not have raincoats. I know that all of these women were not crazy because I used to stop and talk with some of them. Sometimes I sat and drank with them in the park. They were always glad to have company once they got over their suspicions. When I wore my old jeans, construction work boots, and a tattered canvas jacket, I blended in well. These women were as sane as I. Our primary difference was that I had enough money to cope with the problems that befell me and they did not. When I got fed up with people, I could take a vacation. If I got depressed, I could go to Bloomingdale's. When I needed someone to talk to I could hire a psychotherapist. Where I could hire a lawyer to fight for me if I were treated unjustly, these women could only rant and scream—though on occasion, ranting and screaming worked well enough for them to get a bite to eat or a cup of coffee.

On cold days, I sometimes bought them booze so that they could feel warm and escape their misery for a while. They never asked for much. A pair of new high-top sneakers was the only substantial request that was ever made of me. A cup of coffee or something to eat was usually all they ever requested. Often they talked about their families. The ones who had families were very proud of their families. I could not understand how their families could leave them to languish in the streets, but they did.

Much to my son's chagrin, some of these women would call him by name and approach him when they saw him walking down the street and ask him how he was doing, whether I was with him or not. On occasion my son would run errands after school for an old Italian man who ran a small sandwich shop, pizza parlor and grocery store with a video arcade in back. This man would reward my son with quarters which he predictably used to play the video machines. I could never get my young son to see that he was working for free. Frequently the old crones would follow my son into the sandwich shop so that they could give me a report on what they saw. They generally provided an accounting as to how many video games he had played and how many slices of pizza he had eaten.

My son viewed these women with suspicion because frequently they were dirty and unkempt, but I knew that they would not harm him. Frequently one of these women would meet me at the subway to give me a report on what my son had done on his way home from summer classes. Although I did not always understand why these women did what they did, I did understand that they were desperately poor and trying to survive on the streets of Manhattan.

That any woman who has spent years of her life raising a family should come to such a bad end is a travesty. In spite of all the lip-service that our society gives to motherhood, woe unto the mothers who cannot provide for themselves in their old age. Thousands are placed on the street corners of America every day, like so many sacks of garbage, only for these women there is no daily pick up. And so they languish. For these women, catching a man was indeed only a temporary solution. Unless we improve the lot of women, many will continue to languish.

I have been away from Manhattan for three years now. I often wonder if my old friends are dead or alive. There was no way to keep in touch with them since they lived without addresses on street corners, in parks, and in alleyways. They do, however, still live in my heart, most particularly the kind and loving Sadie, who was truly a gentle woman in spite of her booming voice, wild-eyed and snaggle-toothed laugh, and thoroughly frightful appearance.

She was almost 6 feet tall and weighed well over 200 pounds. Her hair was almost all white and when she did not comb it, which was often, it stood straight on edge. She was fond to wear high-topped sneakers which only added to her garish appearance. Those who did not know her would move out of the way when they saw her coming. Those who knew her were always glad to see that Sadie was still alive as she had numerous medical problems. I always saw her as a warm-hearted, big, black mother earth who had love for everyone. However, unlike the picture book earth-mothers, she was just a little dirty and just a little torn.

The last time I saw her she was nervously waiting to have surgery. She was afraid of hospitals, but was always glad to see the doctors and nurses who were kind to her. It saddens me to think of her still wander ing the streets of New York, but she is a survivor in a world that is known for its cruelty to women, most especially the poor women who hold the last places in the line for individual remedies. As always, by the time the pot reaches the last pair of hands, there is nothing left.

Chapter 6

The Hazards of Clinging to the Old Ways

The *Black Man's Guide*, like many who idealize "the good-old days," was quick to draw upon the legend of the romantic yesteryear when men were real men, women were real women, and men kept their women in their places. The author tells us that in every country in the world, including black countries, women rightfully recognize the right of the men to rule and bow down accordingly. Supposedly, in these countries the men can prosper because they have their women under control. Curiously, the author fails to discuss these other black countries except: (1) to make disdainful comments about black American women dressed in traditional African garb and sporting dreadlocks and (2) to allude to the pride and prowess of the African male and the control he has over his women.

One would assume that the African male who has his woman in check and sits on the throne as king would prosper and have world respect, but this is not so. Blacks, whether African or Afro-American or Afro-Caribbean or whatever, are held in disrepute in most countries throughout the world. If black men have it so great in these non-American countries, it is amazing that they continue to flock to America where black men are held in such disrepute and where any man with dark skin is likely to be viewed as a black American since all blacks look alike. Many black men who come to America from Africa and the Caribbean work two or three jobs at a time so that they can send money back home to needy families. Truly these men have not prospered in their black homelands.

The harsh conditions under which non-American blacks labor was brought home to me by a thirty-five-year-old African male named Obi. When I had occasion to serve an externship working for a black Federal District Court judge, Obi was convicted of heroin smuggling. He was a balloon swallower, i.e., he smuggled the heroin in a number of small balloons that he had swallowed. The pre-sentencing report revealed that Obi had a college degree and a good prospect for going on to medical school. For more than seven years he had worked two jobs to support his family in Africa while attending a California community college at night. His ultimate goal was to work until he had the funds to attend medical school.

Shortly after Obi finished his undergraduate degree and was hired by a defense contractor, he was laid off. Because Obi had forty-three relatives in Nigeria to support, he could not afford to wait to be recalled, which ironically would have been ninety days later. After seven years of labor he had only two hundred dollars in the bank. An African drug dealer who knew of Obi's predicament talked him into swallowing some heroin-filled balloons and attempting to smuggle the contraband into the United States to make some quick money. Obi was caught and did not have the funds for bail. No friends or family came to his rescue. A kind-hearted white law professor, who frequently visited the court and was well known and well respected by all the Federal Court judges, represented Obi *pro bono*, but little could be done as Obi was caught with the drugs in his intestines.

During my tenure with the judge, who had a reputation for being tough on criminals, Obi was the only criminal I saw the judge cringe on sentencing. Obi was a good man, desperate for funds, who made a foolish mistake. Obi's biggest crime was being born poor. However, the new federal sentencing guidelines give the judge no discretion in meting out sentences. Obi received a stiff sentence and will now never be able to attend medical school. His young nieces and nephews in Africa can no longer pay their school tuition without Obi's assistance and his fiance will not be able to join Obi in America. Obi's confinement throws the entire family into jeopardy.

In spite of their so-called dominion over their women, many non-American black men like Obi cannot prosper in the black countries into which they are born because of the corrupt black governments that bleed the black populace dry. This is not to say that all black governments are corrupt, but instead, that they are as corrupt as white governments. The white man did not teach us to lie and to steal. Black governments have proved no more benevolent than white governments. Greed is a universal trait that is not limited to white men.

Having dominion over their women is a superficial remedy that has not saved and cannot save black men anywhere. Black men should seek to control their governments, not their women. Blacks will not be saved until the root of the problem is remedied—our systems of government that allow the powerful few to dominate the powerless many.

In spite of the "respect and honor" the *Black Man's Guide* tells us is accorded non-American black men by their women and in spite of the fact that they are "allowed to come first," all men with dark skin continue to be disadvantaged by the color of that skin. In spite of our many tongues, our universal classification is nigger.

In many instances and in spite of the low status of American blacks, non-American blacks fare far worse than American blacks. In some Caribbean countries, every boat docked in the scenic harbor belongs to a white man, though all those operating the boats are black men. I once visited an old sugar cane plantation in the Caribbean where blacks (whole families) were still living in the old one-room slave quarters. Harlem looked like heaven compared to these quarters. In some European countries, at the trendy discos, any black who does not look American or who cannot produce an American passport is routinely turned away at the door, much as American blacks are routinely turned away from the trendy New York City discos.

Having their women in check and being treated like kings by their women has done little to improve the status or condition of many non-American blacks. The domination of black women has not proved to be an effective combatant to racism or served to increase the stature of the black male any place in the world. In every foreign country in which I have travelled, whether the country was black-ruled or white-ruled, I have generally received better treatment than local blacks but only because I was an American. In some places I have received better treatment than I have in my own country. As much as I despise the racial politics of America, I know that my American passport has saved me much grief and that many would trade an arm or a leg for an American passport.

Those who think that their lot in life will improve if only they can control the black woman are apt to be disappointed down the line. The problem is not in the black male or the black female but in how others have been conditioned to perceive us. We cannot change that perception by changing ourselves because many of the perceptions whites have of us are totally irrational. It is whites, not blacks, who must change to eliminate racism. All blacks can do is make sure that we are prepared to fight a good battle, whether in the classroom, the boardroom, the courtroom, or any place in the market.

The *Black Man's Guide* also fails to tell us why, with all this magnificent male leadership inspired by female submission, the world is still so screwed up. In almost every country in the world, including America, people are without food and shelter and are dying of disease. What is so great about any of our systems of government if one is a have not in a system of haves? Change is long overdue. The old days and the old ways are precisely what many of us are trying to escape.

The old ways of natural superiority theories are fraught with danger. For example, if male dominance is better, is not white male dominance better yet? After all, the white man has certainly kicked ass. The old ways must be challenged and changed, by both the oppressor and the oppressed, or the minority community's very survival may be threatened.

For the black community, shutting our eyes to the realities of 1991 and clinging to the old ways that enabled grandma and grandpa to survive, often by sacrificing their human dignity bit by bit, will not ensure the survival of the large numbers of urban black youth who must cope with drugs that did not exist in the days of grandma and grandpa, vicious gangs, and drive-by shootings. For many of these youths, the immediate problem is surviving in their own neighborhoods, not dealing with the white man. Many never live to confront "the man," unless L.A.P.D., N.Y.P.D., or some other big-city police department rolls into the neighborhood. Instead these black youths' immediate battles are with other black men (or would-be men) in their communities. Nor will shutting our eyes to the reality of the inequities in rural communities ensure the survival of the black rural youth who, like his big-city counterpart, may have been born into circumstances devoid of any human dignity to sacrifice that will ensure survival. Racist whites who were once content to have blacks call them "sir" or to have blacks step aside so that whites could pass by first are no longer so easily mollified.

For some black youths, becoming more inhumane is the only option they can see to ensure their survival. "Don't mess with him, he's crazy," is universally understood, whether "he" is a cold-blooded dope dealer or a 250-pound man wearing a dress and waving an American flag. I had often wondered why pimps make spectacles of themselves by wearing outrageously garish clothing and driving cars that look like something out of Dick Tracy comic books until a pimp explained to me that looking outrageous is the whole point. That way, the clients come to the pimp, as do the prostitutes, even the sixteen-year-olds who profess their innocence. (According to his theory what the sixteen-year-olds do not know is that they will be treated like every other prostitute. Somehow these young girls think that because they are special or different, the rules will be different for them. Sadly, such is not the case. A pussy is just a pussy.) A pimp can easily ply his trade by sitting in his parked car without ever opening his mouth because everyone in America knows what the deal is.

Many young black men who know what the deal is in their gang-infested neighborhoods know that they will not survive in these blighted and crime-infested communities unless they get tougher and crazier than the next guy. If one youth pulls out a club, another youth pulls out a knife. If one youth pulls a knife, another pulls a gun. One youth shoots two people, another shoots six. This is perfectly logical, however mad. The game is survival in a world of madness. No doubt if the old-line, die-hard segregationists had had uzis and BMW's instead of ropes, horses, and shotguns, grandma and grandpa would not have survived their onslaught either. Therefore, it is shortsighted to look to the old ways to save many of our extremely troubled modern youth, be they male or female, from the problems they face every day.

In the days of slavery, blacks had no control over their lives. Their every act was controlled by whites—whether, when and if they would eat, drink, multiply, live or die. Blacks were forced to develop coping mechanisms to deal with this truly unnatural circumstance. Fortunately, such is no longer the case. Unfortunately, some of the coping mechanisms that were developed by blacks to allow us to cope with the slave market are inadequate to cope with the current capitalist market, where one seldom confronts other people but instead must deal with bureaucratic systems of mazes. Those who cannot run the mazes are swept out into the streets—young, old, male, female, deaf, dumb, blind, cripple, and crazy. One's circumstances are irrelevant in these bureaucratic mazes as there is no one to listen. Under these harsh conditions, blacks can no longer afford to retreat from battles, nor content ourselves to wait for things to get better. As many of our brave ancestors forged ahead in the face of every adversity, *all* of us must forge ahead today.

In the 1600's, black men and women in America had no choice except to greet each day without long-term plans and commitments but with the hope that a higher power would provide a future because they had absolutely no control over their own bodies, let alone the future. Each day could well bring the last time one saw daylight or his or her children or loved ones. One even had to be careful about hoping for the demise of the old master as the new master might be even crueler. The daily uncertainty of being a log adrift at sea must have brought excruciating agony to those who yearned for their freedom but could not fight the master's dogs, whips, chains, guns, and laws. The laws were the cruelest of all. They kept one in bondage even without chains.

In the 1900's, black men and women who greet each day without a long-range plan and a backup plan in case the first plan does not work will find survival difficult, if not impossible. In our throw-away society one can quickly go to ruin in a single day's time. If the toaster no longer works, we throw it out. If a shirt of dress no longer fits, we throw it out. If a spouse no longer fits, we throw the spouse out, too. Anything that fails to function gets thrown out. Ours is not a society where one can afford not to exercise every limited power one has. It is too easy to be thrown out with the garbage when one appears non-functional. One who fails to exercise the power that he or she does have will soon lose even that.

Strangely, many blacks do not make maximum use of our newly found freedom and limited power. Many are so used to having to take a back seat that we do so automatically, without being told. As a great observer of youth I am often aghast at their behavior. I have watched many get onto the bus and head straight to the back without being told that such is their place, as it has been historically. In fact, these youngsters prefer to sit there, operating under a delusion that they have taken it over or that it is their territory, when in reality the back was carved out for them over three hundred years ago. Even today, one can watch many whites on the bus stand in the aisles even though there are empty seats in the back. For some reason, they simply refuse to sit in the back. I often wonder what the whites who refuse to sit in the back would do if all blacks started to sit in the front of the bus. Would the back become more acceptable if blacks no longer sat there, much as, with urban renewal, the inner cities become more acceptable when blacks no longer live there?

Watching some black youths on the New York City subways is a painful experience. Some will push and shove for the privilege of riding on the last cars, the gangster cars, because as they see it, there they can break all the subway rules and regulations and no one dares to complain. It is their car all right. Only tourists and fools dare to hop onto the back cars when the rowdy teenagers, like demons from hell, swoop out from the classrooms in which they are caged during the daylight hours.

"Never get on the last car" is whispered to new initiates of the subway a thousand times a day. On hearing these words, most visitors to New York City nod knowingly. No one has to say, "because all the niggers are in the back." As if there were ethers in the air, everyone who hears the message not to ride in the back cars somehow automatically knows why it is not safe to ride there, even those from foreign countries who can barely speak English.

I doubt that even vigilante Bernard Goetz was foolish enough to plant himself as a decoy on the last car while on his touted search-and-destroy mission, for there, his arsenal of weapons might not have protected him. The last car is for those looking to cut loose, for those who rock the house and figure they will rock the subway, too, if they can get away with it. One frequently observes these same youths in the back row at the movie theaters talking more loudly than the moving picture.

For some reason these youths always seem to travel en masse. Thus, those who seek to challenge these youths must be willing to confront six to eight teenagers at a time. Though it has been my experience that many of these teens will at least listen to what their challengers have to say before cursing them out, and some will slink away in shame when asked if their mothers know how they act in public, the fact that these youths travel in packs generally discourages all but the foolhardy from approaching them.

The last time I had occasion to challenge such a group was out of necessity as I had the misfortune of being seated next to them as they proceeded to roll a whole bag of joints to smoke in the movie theater. They were outraged at my suggestion that they smoke their dope some place else and that it was they who should move and not I since I was doing nothing illegal. They gave me an ear full as they got up and moved, but I know that they were basically good kids or they would have stomped me into the ground to boot. These children need to be corrected before they develop habits that they cannot break or become entangled with the police and become statistics. Had I been a cop, all of them would now have records over simple-minded foolishness.

It baffles me that one has but to create a hell hole, and many of our youths magically take a place there, as if they were enticed there by some mysterious ether. Are we so used to being beaten down that we just naturally assume the rear position without being told? I can understand the older generation feeling beaten down, but how has the younger generation so quickly picked up on this defeat?

In 1991, it is no longer illegal for blacks to pursue an education; blacks can vote if registered; and in many instances, blacks can live wherever they can afford to live. And yet on a visit to many public schools that have been integrated, one can generally see some black students vie for the back row where they sit and play games instead of paying attention to what is being taught in class. While they may think themselves rebellious, they are actually doing just what the system that they are blind to wants them to do. No one has told these children that they have to sit in the back row and act like clowns. They sit there automatically, making fun of the black students who do try to learn. These misguided students are just as dangerous as racist whites (perhaps more so since they do not appear to be the enemy and may therefore ensnare more black youth before their unwary cohorts see the trap) in that they discourage other black students from learning.

Even though they are only children, the offending black students should be sternly taken to task. Black male students are particularly prone to assume the attitude that it is not cool to be smart. No doubt this is part of the reason for their disproportionate dropout rate and failure to excel academically. These students generally have a million excuses for their behavior. For their own inability to sit still and pay attention for 50 minutes at a time, they blame everyone from the white man to their own mothers and fathers, to the girl in the short skirt.

That they might be able to exercise internal self-control is not within their realm of thinking. They see everything in their lives as being controlled by someone or something else. They can only react, not act. They do not see that once the school game is over and they are held fully accountable as adults, excuses will not buy bread or support their families or keep them out of jail.

In the much harsher game of life, these young people are generally surprised to find that the ante has been upped. The same adults who used to pat them on the heads and call them cute will now snarl at them viciously. The old dogs resent the competition from the new dogs on the block and will guard their territory jealously. Where before the young pups were playfully slapped when they misbehaved, now they are bitten hard. Many will be mauled and some will not survive the game. Even the most mild-mannered players will be playing for blood. Excuses no longer count, even valid ones. Before one is gonged and swept away from the video game of life, ten other players are there fighting to get on the same machine. The students who played around in school are generally the losers in the new, much harsher game. Many will never be given another opportunity to learn.

All too often, the black students who try to learn in school are criticized and made fun of by their black peers, not their white ones. Too often, the message to black students from their black peers is that it is not "cool" to be too smart. Many black teenagers will let their grades drop to be part of the crowd. It is so easy to blame the crowd instead of accepting responsibility for self and taking control of one's life.

If not for the seriousness with which the statements are generally offered, it would be ludicrous to listen to grown adults blame their failure to exercise self-control on Satan or the forces of evil, instead of on themselves. As with many of our youth, these adults have numerous excuses not to take control or not to admit that a conscious deliberate choice was made to act inappropriately. One would think that we were still operating under the institution of slavery where blacks had no reason to think they had control over anything because clearly, they did not. Tragically, no one need hold the reigns from us where we fear to take them. We have been conditioned well.

It is distressing that some choose not to take advantage of the opportunities to exercise internal control, but instead wait for some external power to take control. Often when I have approached black friends or acquaintances about voting, or getting involved in issues that disproportionately affect blacks, or even about educating our young children, I have been told, "You're worried about the things of this life. I'm not worried about the things of this world. I'm worried about everlasting life!"

The speaker generally assumes a haughty and self-righteous air, as if this were an honorable and righteous position that merited strong approval. This position is a sorry cop-out. All who live in this world are subject to its laws, whether or not they choose to heed them. If one chooses not to obey the laws, most assuredly he or she will be locked up, as the legal system in America has yet to recognize everlasting life as a system of higher jurisprudence or anything else.

Today, young people must be extra careful of the legal system because where once young offenders were given a chance to join the military or job corps, today they go straight to jail. Under the new federal sentencing guidelines *where there is no longer routine parole*, many young black men with a single previous misdemeanor conviction are shocked to find that on their first felony convictions, their sentences may be almost doubled because of their prior criminal history. Twenty years with no probation is a long time, even for those who are not concerned about this life or the things of this world. I have watched as even the most hard-hearted of young men have had to fight to hold back the tears when their friends and families hear the judge pronounce twenty years. Those who receive forty years seem almost unable to rise from their chairs in spite of how tough they were on the streets.

The argument frequently bandied about that one should learn to live in this world but not of this world is of a similar ilk. Yet few of the advocates of ignoring worldly things profess to give up eating or sex or putting locks on their doors because these are worldly acts. Clever plays on words make for good rhetorical debates but have little practicality for have-not's in the world of have's, where one's choices are limited to the amount of money one has. Advising inexperienced, poor, young people not to concern themselves with the things of this world, assures that these young people will remain poor, in addition to leaving them with no coping strategies to effectively deal with living in modern times where one is only a face in a bureaucratic system of mazes.

A young teen who is approached to join a gang can hardly tell a crew of thugs that he lives in this world but not of this world and still survive within the neighborhood in which he has been trapped like a rat since birth. There have been no reports yet of divine intervention stopping any group of gang-bangers from beating some poor kid half to death who refused to join the gang. Arming the kids who do not want to join gangs (gangs that are armed with sub-machine guns) with clever semantic and tautological arguments, telling these kids to have faith and be of good cheer, and sending them back to neighborhoods in which even the so-called men of God are afraid to live is sending these kids to their deaths. They need help now, not next week, next month, next year or in the next world.

The semantic, religious and philosophical debates may be forever waged. The point is not whose religion or philosophy is right or wrong but that these arguments all too often impede black progress. Waiting for divine inspiration or the revolution to save us has proved fruitless. After almost four hundred years we are still niggers. Many blacks today are in a worse predicament than they were twenty years ago. Whether we like or accept the system, we must do something to survive besides wait for help to arrive, most particularly since we appear to be in the midst of the Second Reconstruction.

The current conservative white backlash seems hell bent on overturning forty years of legislation and taking us back to the 1950's. If we are content to sit and wait, most assuredly we will be taken back to the 1950's. Ours is a country where the majority rules. The majority decides what is right and what is wrong. What is morally right or wrong is irrelevant in a system where majority rules. Contrary to popular belief, the law is not based on absolute moral principles. The law is based merely on what the majority deems is appropriate under the circumstances.

Few of us can afford to think that because we have gotten our slice of the pie we are safe in a world where empires routinely fall with a drop in the stock market or a hint of scandal. Those who have yet to get a slice of anything should be truly outraged and should express their outrage in a forum other than their own neighborhoods. A lot more can be accomplished by standing on the corner of city hall rather than on the corner in one's neighborhood, even if one should choose merely to stand there and drink wine. Any time a dozen "Negroes" stand on one corner in a predominantly white area, some authority figure will try to figure out what the problem is. Unfortunately, as long as all the human misery is hidden away in isolated black communities, society need never address it. As with discrimination, if white America does not see the problem, the problem does not exist. The reality of ten million people is irrelevant.

In the days when I was active with the NAACP, I never ceased to be amazed at the number of black people who had never contributed a dime to the organization or come to a single meeting but who nonetheless were the first to ask for help when they fell victims to disastrous discrimination. Few of us can afford not to support organizations such as the NAACP, the Urban League, Operation PUSH or some other organization devoted to protecting our interests.

Those who represent our interests need our votes and support to win battles. Who gets into office is determined by whom we vote for, or all too often, whom we fail to vote for. Politics may be a dirty game, but for the moment, it is the only game in town. Blacks who do not vote are just dead weight that the community must carry. Those who do not vote need not complain of racism because they are not even in the game. Likewise, those who do not educate their children can hardly complain when their children cannot find jobs as their children cannot get into the game either.

It is understandable that during the time of slavery when blacks had no control over anything, including their own bodies, they would look to external forces to save them. However, a similar attitude in 1991 ignores four hundred years of history. There has been no one to save us except when we have taken to the streets to save ourselves. The Civil

War was not fought because of a concern that slavery was immoral. President Lincoln himself wrote that if slavery would bind the states into one strong union then he too would support slavery. In a letter to the editor of the *New York Tribune*, Lincoln wrote:

> ... If there be those who would not save the Union unless they could at the same time destroy slavery, I do not agree with them. My paramount object in this struggle is to save the Union, and is not either to save or to destroy slavery. If I could save the Union without freeing any slave, I would do it; and if I could save it by freeing all the slaves, I would do it; and if I could save it by freeing some and leaving others alone, I would also do that. What I do about slavery and the colored race, I do because I do believe it helps to save the Union.[44]

The interests of the "colored race" have always been subjugated to the interests of white America.

Of the many blacks who took to the streets and died there, many hoped only that their sacrifice would help other blacks live a better life. The legions of Medgar Evers and Fannie Lou Hamers did not put their lives on the line so that present day blacks could be well supplied with Jheri-curls and spandex. For those of us who have reaped a single benefit or have only the mere prospect to reap a single benefit, to sit back and profess non-concern for this world is an outrage and utmost hypocrisy.

I used to have a friend who would enrage me by his frequent comment that Ronald Reagan was the best thing that ever happened to black people in America because if Ronnie didn't wake us up, nothing would. Though I have tried, I have been unable to get his words out of my mind. Reagan has come and gone but the awakening is slow. Are we so beaten down that we cannot get up?

My all-time hero in life was a black man who could not read or write, nicknamed Slim because he looked like a beanpole. He proved to me that black people can get up. Like my father, Slim grew up in the South. After Slim's family was abandoned by his father, young Slim at age thirteen hopped a freight train with only a sack lunch and a change of clothing in search of work so that he could provide for his mother and sister who were destitute. He hoboed from someplace in Mississippi (I believe), eventually reaching Chicago. Along the way, he slept in hobo camps or by roadsides taking any job offered for however long it took so that he could send money to his mother. Often he had to depend upon the kindness of the men in the hobo camps for scraps of food.

After several years in Chicago, Slim managed to save enough to move his mother and sister to Chicago. By then he was in his twenties and became concerned that if he did not find a wife soon he might never find one. He married a beautiful Junoesque woman named Annie Mae, who already had five children by her first husband, who had long since abandoned her. She was working in a potato chip factory, peeling potatoes, desperate to make ends meet when she met Mr. Slim. Eventually Slim and Annie had three more children. Mr. Slim treated all the children as his own. As time passed, Mr. Slim squirreled away enough money for a candy store, where Annie and the children worked while he worked other jobs.

Eventually Slim bought a two-story house with a basement for the large family. Some of the by then adult children fell on hard times so Annie and Slim raised some of their grandchildren, too. When Mr. Slim retired, he bought a home in Michigan hoping that he and Annie could be happy away from the big city. The house in Chicago was left to his youngest daughter, who had four children by a husband who had abandoned her.

The upkeep of both houses was difficult and Mr. Slim was forced to come out of retirement to make ends meet. Because he had never owned a car and neither he nor Annie had ever learned how to drive, Mr. Slim was limited to taking a job within walking distance. Well into his sixties, he took a job at a lumber mill that was four or five miles away from his Michigan home so that he could walk to work. He worked about five or so more years frequently walking home at dusk. Then he discovered he had cancer.

Annie was distraught that her husband who had worked so hard would die never having enjoyed his retirement. Slim survived his cancer surgery, but soon afterwards, Annie died of a stroke. Slim was heartbroken but continued his chemotherapy treatments and was cured. Though he outlived his wife by five or six years, he never remarried. For him, no other woman could ever hold a candle to his Annie Mae or was fit to sit at her table.

Mr. Slim encouraged anyone who would listen to get the education that he never had the opportunity to pursue. He almost lived to see his youngest son receive his Ph.D. Often when I watched Slim work in his garden, I saw him become frustrated when he had to stop work to get someone to read him the instructions on a bag of fertilizer or weed killer. He was a very careful man. He would tromp into the kitchen holding a large sack of some chemical and lay it on the table for Annie to read the instructions to him. After fussing about the table, she always obliged. He would always say thank you before going back to the garden. He remembered her every word, even the misread ones, just as she had read them. If Slim had gotten an education, who knows what he would have been able to do. As it was, this illiterate man died debt-free, owning two homes. He raised eight children and four or five grandchildren. When I think of him, I am saddened that such a kind and loving gentleman knew only hard work, but I feel great inspiration. He was a man who had nothing and no chance, yet turned his life and the lives of those dear to him around. Except for his dear wife, Annie, no one ever lifted a finger to help Slim.

When I see black youth who drop out of school because they are too lazy to go or because school is a drag, I think that it is a pity that they did not know Slim. At the same time, I am angered by their stupidity. I am angry to think of the many black men like Mr. Slim who have had to give up so much and work so hard just to survive. If Slim had had half the opportunity young people today have, he would not have died illiterate. Today's black youths are simply going to have to assume more responsibility for themselves. It is plain irresponsible not to finish school in 1991.

I cannot understand the attitude of so many youth that success means wearing a suit and tie and driving a BMW even though they have not a clue as to what they will do to pay for either. I am continually perplexed as to why so many of the blacks with whom I am well acquainted define "success" only in terms of a white-collar profession. Mr. Slim was one of the most successful men I have ever known. I never saw him wear a suit except when he was going to a funeral.

I have tried to encourage many young people to go into the building trades, but many view the building trades or any manual labor with disdain, even those who can barely make ends meet. I cannot get young people to see that one can acquire more self-esteem from being able to pay one's bills, than one can ever acquire from a suit of clothing. There are few jobs in America that do not require a college education that pay as well as the building trades.

Not surprisingly, some local unions do require a college education. For example, Local #3 in New York City requires a two-year degree in addition to a lengthy apprenticeship. In the future, other jurisdictions will likely join Local #3's ranks as more and more people realize the advantages of belonging to a well paying union. Many of the electricians I worked with in New York City were ex-teachers and engineers who found the electrical trade more lucrative than the positions they had previously held.

Those black students who think that they will play around in high school and then straighten up and go to college, or play around in college and then straighten up and go to a graduate or professional school can forget it. The competition is too stiff. A so-called good law school will typically receive around six thousand applications per year but limit entry to around three hundred students. These schools can easily select an entire class with a perfect 4.0 GPA. Even graduating summa cum laude does not assure one of a place in a top graduate or professional school where summa cum laude's are a dime a dozen.

The myths presented in the white media that unqualified minorities can find academic acceptance because of their skin color are just that— myths. The black youths who buy into these myths are in for a bitter disappointment when the doors of academia are slammed in their black faces. Even though statistically the numbers are not great, there are enough minorities in the market who have graduated from Ivy League Schools or have perfect or nearly perfect GPA's or perfect or nearly perfect scores on various entrance exams to ensure that the competition among minorities is as keen as competition among any racial group. Sadly, a "C" is a ticket to nowhere.

Those students who choose not to buckle down or who labor under such great financial and personal hardship that budgeting time for study is almost an impossibility should feel no shame in a blue-collar career. These students should be forewarned that even many blue collar careers require one to devote years to some type of consistent study and to be able to do well on exams. Of the twelve electrical apprentices in the class with which I started, at least half of us had a couple of years of college before getting into the trade. The same was true of many of the other trades, in particular the pipe and steamfitters, the other so-called prima donna trade. Redneck or not, some of the men in these trades are not dummies or slackers. These days, there is no escaping competition, whether in a white-collar or blue-collar profession.

Those black students who cannot or who choose not to go on to college should think about preparing themselves for a skilled trade. Many of these trades take years to break into; therefore, one cannot wait for years to get started. There is no shame in sweating for a living. I for one am always proud to walk past a building that I as a journeyman electrician helped to erect. It is an unparalleled thrill to view the building standing tall in the skyline of a city while one flies overhead in a commercial aircraft. Most of these buildings will be around years after those who constructed them have passed away. Every light that I see in the skyline of any major city tells me that some electrician's family ate well. I encourage black females as well as black males to break into the building trades. One no longer has to be part of a father and son team to gain admission, but one may have to fight.

Troubled by the absence of black faces in all of the building trades, I once wrote to a popular black women's magazine asking why they did not encourage more black women to go into construction. I received a terse reply that the editors felt that in light of the uncertain economy, construction appeared to be an unstable industry that did not offer a secure future for blacks "unless you know something that we don't know."

I never responded to the letter because one week later I moved to New York and was thereby overwhelmed with adjustments, but in retrospect, what career or industry is stable? Many of the white-collar workers who treated me royally when I had the pleasure of working with them in various computer rooms and on various trading floors of several monolithic New York brokerage houses are now pounding the pavement looking for jobs. When I initially encountered these white collar workers, after myself having spent years working outside in the cold, in manholes with frozen slime, and out of bucket trucks, I thought white-collar workers had it made.

At Merrill Lynch, I was always flabbergasted at the twice daily arrival of the tea carts containing three or four kinds of bagels and fruits; an assortment of sweet pastries from a young child's dream; an assortment of jellies, jams, teas, coffees and cheeses; my favorite, boiled eggs; and an assortment of milks and juices from which one had unlimited choice. On occasion we were also treated to "box lunches." Merrill's idea of a box lunch was a beggar's delight.

When I had occasion to work at NBC, a major TV network headquartered in Rockefeller Center, I discovered that some of the employees there had a similar arrangement. Because of an explosion and fire in a manhole under the street that put the TV network's electrical service in jeopardy, we worked around the clock—overtime heaven. At break time, we often received trays of roast beef, ham, and turkey sandwiches and cartons of sodas even as we worked in the streets, so that delays would be minimized. We were often treated to dinner in one of the NBC cafeterias for employees. Generally there were at least three entrees; several side dishes and salads; an assortment of bread and cheese; fruits; an assortment of desserts; and several kinds of ice cream. None of the construction workers, myself included, could believe that any employer treated its employees so generously.

But while I was under the computer floors working with my tools, many of the white-collar workers I had met were being given pink slips and escorted from the building. For many, it was a humbling experience to realize that they too could be laid off like common workers. I had been laid off on so many occasions that a pink slip did not bother me. It just meant that I had to find another job, which I always did.

The unheralded layoffs America is experiencing are likely to continue as long as the United States remains the largest debtor country in the world. Job changes and career changes are a new requirement for survival in the marketplace. Those who cannot change accordingly will be pushed into the growing ranks of the homeless. Many of the homeless are simply workers who have lost their jobs—not a bunch of crazies and lazies. There is no job security for anyone in America these days, except perhaps the undertakers, until we do something about our overblown budget. No doubt the multi-billion dollar cure will take decades.

In retrospect, I also should have responded to the magazine editor that the construction industry has always been a cyclical industry and probably always will be. The wages are high in part because there generally is not year-round work unless one is willing to travel to another jurisdiction to work. Nonetheless, a person who gets into one of the trades and lives modestly can survive a lot better than many sitting behind desks wearing white collars.

All seven of my sisters and brothers have at least one college degree, but as an electrician, I made much more than every single one of them. I may have had to work harder and been subject to more slings and arrows of outrageous misfortune but financially, I was in a much better position than many people I knew with college degrees, especially those who graduated from less well-ranked schools.

The electrical trade made a big difference in my son's childhood experiences as contrasted with my childhood experiences. At age eighteen, I had never been outside of the state of Texas. At age fifteen, my son has travelled around the world. He is as comfortable with his passport as he is with his school identification card. In fact, he is a better traveller than I in that the exchange rates never confuse him. When we travelled to a country with three different exchange rates, my son kept himself well supplied with candy, bubble-gum, and pocket change by counting money and making purchases for those Americans in the group who were overwhelmed by the different exchange rates. I can always depend on my son to make sure our money is counted correctly. I know that most parents want their children to be able to do the things that they as children never had the opportunity to do. Because I know it takes money to do these things, it concerns me that so many well-paying job sites have no black faces.

It disturbs me that since the last time I worked in my home local almost ten years ago, only one black person that I know of has applied for an apprenticeship position. He was not accepted, so still, the local has no working black members. (There are two other women now.) And yet there are young blacks in the town who complain that they cannot find work. I suspect that many of them are looking for a job where they can wear a suit and a tie. The mystery is why they hold this expectation in light of the history of blacks in America? Surely they do not think that this is really an equal opportunity society! Have we allowed our own children to become brainwashed by the mindless propaganda of equal opportunity? Are we so anxious to cling to myths that we can deny reality?

In retrospect, I should also have responded to the magazine editor that those who wait for the wagon to move along at a good pace before hopping on will be dismayed to find that it can take from five to eight years to complete an apprenticeship and that by the time one's apprenticeship is completed, the wagon may have slowed down again. Actually, it is better to start one's apprenticeship in the lean years because when presented with the choice of laying off a journeyman who is making twenty-five dollars per hour and an apprentice who is making twelve dollars per hour, most contractors will lay off every journeyman they are allowed to lay off before laying off a single apprentice. In fact, if not for the business agents at the union halls who keep an eye on the contractors, many contractors faced with layoff decisions would retain only apprentices, as contractors tend to be more concerned with making a profit on the job under their noses than with training workers for the future.

Despite the cyclical nature of the work, if not for the electrical trade, I would have perished long ago. In spite of the many trying circumstances which I have had to face, including being beaten senseless and raped on one of the very jobs on which I worked, I have fared far better than most single or divorced black mothers in America. Despite my trials and tribulations, I recommend the electrical trade to any woman because the tide is turning, slowly but surely. True, there is a lot of resistance to women on the job sites, but most contractors have faced enough hardships and law suits to realize that accommodations must be made for women. No woman should stay away from the trades solely because of fear of the unknown.

My own assault and rape should not discourage any other woman either. The entire circumstance could have been prevented but for a stubborn general contractor who refused to provide a rest room or dressing room with a lock on the door for the benefit of one lone female worker. He insisted that if I wanted to be a construction worker I should be a man like everyone else on the job site in spite of the fact that I was not. I have much bitterness in my heart for this man as I could well have lost my life if not for the fact that other electricians on the job site who knew my habits well became alarmed at my disappearance in the middle of the day and stopped work to look for me. They found me beaten unconscious on a rest room floor where I could have lain for days if no one had bothered to check.

Why the man who raped me did not cut my throat with his gleaming knife I will never know. Though he spoke to me, I was so terrified that I could not understand any of the words he spoke. He seemed to grow angrier by the minute. I could see his lips moving and hear his voice, but the words were empty. I could not understand the words he spoke to me because the part of me that could think and understand had separated itself from the part of me that could feel and act. The part of me that could think stood watching him but he did not see her. He saw only the part of me that could feel, the part that lay on the floor, and he continued to speak to her as if the other part were invisible.

The last thing I remember was him pressing against me and squeezing my throat when I dared to try to move away. He would squeeze until I was almost blinded by darkness and then let go. On occasion I had watched cats kill mice the same way. Once the mouse was cornered, the cat would squeeze half the life out of the mouse and then let go. Sometimes the cat would even turn its back to the mouse, while coyly licking the paw fur hiding the razor sharp fangs that were throbbing for the kill. Without turning its head, the cat would continue to peer at the mouse out the corner of one of its slanted, glowing eyes: cold, steel-gray, and harkening a prehistoric age when mighty hunters were kings. The minute the mouse would try to run, the cat would pounce on it again and squeeze a little harder. It was a curious, deadly game that continued until the cat tired of demanding submission at which point the mouse would be killed. After refusing to submit and being overcome by darkness, I thought that I was dead until a white police officer shook me and I discovered that I could still see. His pale face glowed like a ghost's sheet in the semi-darkness but by his warm smile I knew that he was real.

Even after an ambulance arrived and the attendants tried to help me, I could only hear but not understand. I cannot imagine that the words I attempted to speak made much sense, but the police officers continued to talk to me. I became even more frightened when I sensed that they were only trying to distract me—from what, I did not know. But when I saw their guns, I knew that as long as I stayed in the room with them I was safe. For the moment, the small room where I lay was the one spot in the world where I knew I was safe. When the ambulance attendants tried to place me on the stretcher, I knew that they planned to take me from the room and I did not want to go. They appeared baffled at my resistance. I had no intention of leaving the only place in the world where I knew I was safe. I became more and more frustrated. I could see one police officer whispering. I was surrounded by talking heads, none of which I could understand.

Shortly thereafter, to my surprise, a lady cop entered the room. I remember thinking that she looked so small in her black uniform, but she too sported a big gun and I felt safe. She talked to me for quite some time. Her voice was very soothing and some of her words came through. She promised to go to the hospital with me if I would just get onto the stretcher. Eventually I agreed but discovered that I could not get up. She called the attendants and other police back into the room and they carefully loaded me onto the stretcher. The police officers continued to talk to me. Though I could not understand the messages of their voices or their crackling radios, I could feel the kindness in their faces.

For several days afterwards, my mind, like a kind and loyal friend, watched over me even as I slept. When I climbed into bed at night, she sat at the edge, ever watchful. In the mornings, she was still there, as if she did not know the meaning of fatigue. When I felt despair, her gentle smile reassured me.

One morning as I stood in front of the mirror, I stared for quite some time before I realized the reflection in the mirror was mine. As I looked into the glass, I wondered how this strange woman got into my bathroom and why she kept staring at me. Didn't she know that staring was rude? Did she know what had happened to me? Could she tell from looking at me? Would others know? Panic-stricken, I turned from the mirror and bumped into myself. She stood smiling behind me and as always her smile was reassuring. When I looked back into the mirror, I recognized that the reflection was my own. To my surprise, I was able to laugh weakly as I stepped back inside of myself.

For weeks, it seemed that I saw my assailant on every street corner. Sometimes I saw him in my apartment, but being used to dealing with shadows, I knew that I had but to turn on the light and he would evaporate. On days when he was persistent, I would wait until daylight to go to bed.

After years of psychotherapy, I still have a blank spot on my brain about many things that happened that day. However, some things I remember most vividly. I remember that someone called a phone number that was found in my pocket and eventually reached one of my brothers in another state. I remember becoming so furious when the first words out of his mouth were that I should go back to my home in Indiana (ironically, the house whose mortgage payments necessitated my moving to New York) and stop gallivanting all over the country like a man because I was only a woman and women could not do the things men did. His words were a bitter blow!

I could have been killed but all he could think about was keeping me in a woman's place. My hands quivered so, I had to use my left hand to hold my right arm still. I had difficulty maintaining my grip on the telephone receiver. My head began to throb as if it would blow off and my stomach began to churn. I felt the same rage and frustration I had felt when my grandmother and aunt were killed. If my aunt had stayed in her place, perhaps she would be alive today, but then what reason would she have for living—to be a slave to someone else's ego?

Suddenly, I was so fucking furious with the world's dehumanization of women that even though I could barely move and could not control my own shaking, I vowed to myself to get up and fight back! The next time someone kicked me, I would kick back with both feet! I would strike back hard! I would kill the next motherfucker who tried to fuck with my body or my mind! It took me three months to recuperate sufficiently to return to work, but I did return. I will no longer be pushed because I am "only" a woman.

I can write about being raped without tears and rage now, but I cannot hold an articulate conversation in which I must verbalize memories or feeling and confront the rage and humiliation of not being able to control what happened to my own body, even at age thirty-five. I was so sure I had gotten it all together and was on top of my world. I had travelled light years since the first time I experienced rape at age nineteen. Then, I was so poor, naive, and inexperienced that I had great difficulty in controlling what happened to me. But at thirty-five, I thought I had my life all figured out. I had everything—my child, my job, I had decided to finish my undergraduate degree, I had money in the bank, a home, stocks, bonds, everything I could possibly want. I was in control. But to my surprise, I could still be raped. I could still be dominated, as if I were nothing, a body without a mind. To be brought full circle was utterly demoralizing and humiliating. How could life be so unfair. Why me?

Unlike the second assailant, the first was white and I knew who he was. I met him at O'Hare airport when I was stranded during a blizzard there on my way back to school the Christmas my grandmother and aunt were killed. I had been so upset by my aunt's funeral that I could not bring myself to go to my grandmother's funeral. My parent's agreed that it would be best for me to go back to school where I could have some peace and quiet.

I had to transfer planes in Chicago and arrived in the midst of one of the worst snowstorms in Chicago's history, January 1969. It seemed that the plane circled the airport for hours before we could land. I missed my connection as did thousands of other flyers. The airport was packed with people from everywhere who could go nowhere. There were no hotel vacancies in downtown Chicago or in the vicinity of the airport, so the airline booked four of us at a hotel in some unknown suburb.

We went out to the curb to catch a cab and found that there was pandemonium. People were pushing, shoving and screaming to get cabs. I was pushed off the curb and into a puddle of icy water in which my shoes were completely submerged. With all that I had on my mind, I felt crushed by a mere push from the curb. One of the white men in our group helped me up and suggested that we go back inside because at this rate we would never get a cab.

Like frozen zombies, the three of us followed him back inside to the ticket counter. He suggested that the airline ticket agent call a cab from the suburb to which we were going to pick us up, as we had been standing outside in the cold for almost an hour, it was late, and all of us were exhausted. Within the next hour, the cab arrived. I was frozen and fighting back the tears.

The snow continued to fall at an alarming rate and the wind whipped the flakes into a frenzy. While we were en route, twice the cab driver stopped the cab and got out to make sure we were still on the road. An hour later he admitted that we were lost. He told us that he had a full tank of gas and that our best bet was to stay in the cab and keep warm until someone came along who could tell us where we were. He was sure we were on the highway, but not sure where. All of us were concerned that we might be crushed by a big truck, but there was little that we could do. Visibility was limited to about six feet.

Eventually a state trooper showed up. All of us breathed a sigh of relief. The officer escorted the cab to the door of the motel after bawling the cab driver out for being on the road. The ride took about half an hour and all that we could see was the flashing lights on the patrol car about ten feet ahead of us. The highway had been shut down.

I tried with all my might to hold in my anxiety each time the cab skidded across the road. I knew that with all my parents had to deal with, the last thing they needed was for me to be involved in an accident on a highway two thousand miles away. I was thinking about my grandmother and aunt and wondering if the police had caught my uncle yet. I hoped my uncle would not harm my parents. They had looked so old to me after not having seen them for seven months. I was so cold and afraid. I did not want to embarrass myself by crying. I could feel every muscle in my body tense. I started to shake. I did not realize that I was trembling until the white man seated next to me offered his coat.

Once at the motel, he took my bags for me and offered to escort me to my room. He looked respectable, cashmere coat that had the scent of expensive cologne, pin-striped suit, leather attache case, and he carried only a garment bag since he was on a short business trip. I thanked him for the help and allowed him to carry the bags to my room, which turned out to be on the second floor of the two-story motel and at the end of a long pathway.

As he sat my bags down in the room, he asked me if something were wrong. Not wanting to discuss the murders of my grandmother and aunt, I said that nothing was wrong, that I was just tired and cold. He was very witty and a good conversationalist. In spite of my anxiety, I found myself laughing at something he said. Not put off by my stand-off-ishness, he said that if I did not want to talk to him that perhaps a drink would make me feel better, that at least it would warm me up since the desk clerk had warned us that there appeared to be a problem with the heat in the motel.

I repeated that I was just too tired and too cold and he reminded me that I had been wearing wet shoes since my fall from the curb at the airport over three hours ago. I had completely forgotten that my shoes were soaked. He suggested that I put on a dry pair of shoes and accompany him to the bar to have a drink. He promised to escort me back to my room afterwards. When I told him I was too tired to lift the suitcase, he picked up my large suitcase, placed it on the bed, took my keys, opened the suitcase, and took out a pair of shoes. It struck me that he looked so funny standing there in a coat and holding my high-heeled shoes that I began to laugh. He went into the bathroom, came back with a towel, dried my feet and placed the dry pair of shoes on my frozen feet. It was such a relief to have something to laugh about after feeling as though I were living in hell for the past couple of weeks that I accompanied him to the bar.

After a couple of drinks, he escorted me back to my room, said good-night and left. Still cold, I turned up the heat as high as it would go and took a hot shower. When I walked out of the shower, someone grabbed me from behind and covered my mouth. When he pushed me onto the bed, I could see that it was the man I had met in the cab. I could not believe it! He had seemed so kind. He promised not to hurt me if I did not scream. At that point the tears that I had been holding back all day poured forth. Never had I felt so utterly alone, dejected and defeated in my life. This was his territory, not mine.

A million thoughts raced through my head. Would he really hurt me? Would anyone hear me scream? It was futile to scream. No one would take my word over a white man's. Like a fool, I had sat in the bar and had a couple of drinks with this man thinking how nice he seemed. If the police came my parents would be involved. My parents had enough grief and aggravation dealing with the funerals, my cousin, and my normally rational and predictable math professor grandfather, who now laid his gun beside his never absent pencils, and whose parting words to me were to be careful because the world was so wicked.

My angry and grief-stricken grandfather had taken to keeping a double barreled shotgun by the door and a pistol by his bedside. We dared not go to his house without calling him first lest he shoot one of us by mistake. Everything was upside down and crazy. The telephone at my parents' house had not stopped ringing for a week and my parents looked so worn. Surely this was hell.

I remembered the girl down the street who had been raped and how people talked. Her family was so embarrassed that they moved away. I had been warned not to trust white people but I had not listened. My own stupidity had gotten me into this fix. My father would be furious. It was hopeless to continue to struggle as my assailant was so much stronger than I. His well-placed weight and advances were crushing. And so I submitted, silently except for my uncontrollable sobs.

After my assailant discovered that I had never had intercourse before, he was very apologetic, though it did not stop him from finishing the act. Afterwards, he offered to give me money in case I had medical problems. He told me that he had a wife and a family and that he could not afford any trouble. He said that he had just assumed that I had been around and that there would not be any real harm. He repeated that he was sorry over and over like a broken record.

I wanted to yell and scream and throw things, but I could not push him off me. Trembling, I held the rage inside. I did not even know where I was, except that it appeared to be an all white suburb somewhere out in the sticks. I had not seen a black face since leaving the airport and here I lay with nothing to cover me besides a towel, in a motel room with a white man who I knew only by his first name. The very walls, which were also white, seemed to have closed in on me.

Instead of screaming, I told him I did not want his money and begged him to leave, in as calm a fashion as I could. I could feel my nose running and saliva drooling down my face and neck but I could not stop crying. The tears just rolled. I could barely keep my wits about me. He continued to apologize and I continued to ask him to leave. He stared at me for a long time and then he left. As he walked out the door, he reached into his pocket, took out my key and placed it on the table by the door. I had been so stupid at nineteen. I had never missed the key.

But at age thirty-five, I was cautious. I trusted no one. If a stranger on the street asked me if I knew what time it was, I would automatically say no even though I always knew the time because I even slept wearing my watch. And I was always cautious of strangers. The guys on the job used to say that they had never seen a woman who could work all day and never say two words. But I could and frequently I did. At work, I was strictly business and I never dreamed that I could be touched by anything that could wound my very soul.

However, the day I was wheeled off the job on that stretcher, I had been wounded to my very soul. I could feel the eyes of the workers who stood by. Their eyes were touching me. I did not want to see them, nor did I want them to see me. The police kept them back, but I could feel them nonetheless. The ride to the elevator and down four flights was the longest ride of my life. It crossed my mind that death would have been less painful. In subsequent weeks, I had to be careful not to stand too close to the edge of the subway platform as frequently I could hear the tracks whispering to me to come closer. I could not bear to look down. As if being black were not bad enough, there was just no escape from being born a woman.

I can write about rape now because it is much easier to face a blank sheet of paper that yields to my every mood than to face an inquiring human being who does not understand how I feel. I can write about rape because I feel that it is not a personal act against any one woman but against women as a class, much like race discrimination. To the racist, it does not matter whose face is there, but only that the face is black. Likewise I imagine that to the rapist, it does not matter who the woman is, but only that she is a woman. She can be nineteen or ninety, black or white, blind, cripple or crazy. All that matters is that she is a woman. The act is against women, not any one woman. Thus as with racism, individual remedies will not help the masses of women. Women will continue to be preyed upon until the condition of women is remedied.

I am relieved that I no longer spend hours debating with myself whether I should have been more alert or careful or suspicious, or what might or might not have happened if I had been because these debates are fruitless. I accept part of the responsibility for what happened to me but much of the fault I place on the world into which I was born and the place that world reserves for women, the doormats of the world on which all may wipe their feet with impunity. It is a world where no matter how low or to what miserable state of disgrace, despair, or depravity a man has fallen, he still has the "god-given" right to rule a woman, or so he thinks.

Do I blame all men for what happened to me? No. I am eternally grateful to my fellow male workers who cared enough to wonder at my strange absence. In spite of the sexist notions that prevail about women and the racist notions that prevail about blacks, there are many decent men on the construction sites and women can survive there though sometimes survival is hard, damnably hard.

I have learned much of the hazards of myths and clinging to the old ways. I have learned that natural superiority is as mythical as the black knight and equal opportunity. I have learned that in modern times it is dangerous to sacrifice one's dignity and to accept one's place. Such sacrifice only allows more doors to remain closed and more victims to be claimed. I have learned that while I cannot control others, I can control myself. I have learned that if I do not strike back in this life I will continually be knocked for a loop in this life. I have learned that the old ways replicate themselves secretly and asexually, even as we slumber, and silently transplant themselves into our hearts and minds and bodies against our wills. Because they can find nourishment there, they continue to feed and grow rather than to shrivel and to die.

But I have not given up hope because I have also learned that one does not have to be felled by every blow. One can learn to rise up from blows, much as one can learn to walk, to talk, to touch, to feel, to prepare for the marketplace, or to exercise whatever limited power one has in that market. In 1991, blacks, be they male or female, who are slapped down need no longer slink away in silence or wait for times to change. We can rise up and fight back. We no longer have to wait for help that like the revolution never comes. Sometimes it may be necessary to fight with fists, but many times we can fight with books, our minds, attorneys or whatever other resource is within our grasp.

I have also learned that I and other black women need no longer accept oppression from any man, not even from the black men who profess to love us even as they seek to keep us in our place—be they our fathers, co-workers, bosses, brothers or our own sons. Black women can stand up and fight back. Out of poverty, despair, and the ashes of ruination, we can soar—not necessarily like the mighty war hawk, but like the proud birds that we are.

To fight back means that we must live in this world and participate in the activities that will assure us of something concrete, however minimal the reward. Those black men who seek to boost their power and egos at the expense of black women must realize that they are no different from the white oppressors who have sought to and continue to seek to boost their power and egos at the expense of blacks. Both are equally oppressive to the black woman. Those black women who seek only to find a black knight in shining armor in order to escape all responsibility for the conditions of the world must realize that they made the choice, even when the choice turns out badly.

For black women to listen to those who tell us that we need only concern ourselves with finding a black knight, much like the mythical white knight, is shortsighted in light of our history in America. Many who buy into this myth will meet the fate of the blacks who, instead of demanding equality now, listened to the segregationists who promised that things would get better, by and by, someday, if only blacks would wait. While blacks waited, the segregationists retrenched. So strong was the retrenchment that it took the President of the United States of America to knock down the barricades and we have been skirmishing ever since.

The words of Governor Faubus to President Kennedy in defiance of the order to admit the first black student to the University of Arkansas still bounce off the walls of my mind and to this very day still evoke my anger. "We need time, Mr. President," was Governor Faubus' response as to every query as to how much longer. Blacks must wait until whites are ready. Women must wait until men are ready. Sapphire should shut-up until the black man is ready to listen to what she has to say. History repeats itself over and over and over and over because our memories are so short and so, so fickle.

It is unlikely that the current President of the United States is going to knock down any barricades for black women in America. However, in 1991 black women have a choice about which direction we take in life. We no longer have to wait.

Chapter 7

Reflections on Her Sex

Much as racists whites have told us for centuries, the *Black Man's Guide* tells us that "The Black woman spends a great deal of her days and nights being aware of her sexuality. She throbs nearly involuntarily.[45] ...[S]he cannot be trusted in the presence of strange men for a long length of time because she is always open for a line.... Without exception, if a black man pursues her long enough with compliments, flowers, phone calls and the like, she will ultimately go to bed with him."[46] The author fails to tell us how it is possible that those black women who are consumed with the responsibility of families or demanding careers can spend all their time dwelling on sex but maintain their homes and families. Ironically, some of the myths about black female sexuality that have long been perpetuated in the white community have also been perpetuated in the black community.

Whites have not been the only villains in the devaluation of black women. Many black men have also contributed to this devaluation. The most memorable in my personal experience was a black man I worked with shortly before I quit the electrical trade. In my twelve years in the electrical trade I had occasion to curse out only two men. The first was a white man named Gene with whom I eventually became very good friends. The second was a black man named Eddie whom I detest to this day.

Eddie, who was a married man with several children, took great delight in entertaining the men on the job with stories of his exploits with black women. He delighted in telling the crew how to become studs and manipulate women with lies, flattery, and deceit. If Eddie were fifteen minutes late for work in the morning, the construction site grapevine was hot with speculation as to whether or not fate had caught up with him and he had gotten shot crawling out of some woman's bedroom window by her irate husband or lover. Because Eddie was also a traveller (i.e., working outside his home local), his wife was not with him in New York but instead remained in their home in another state. Though everyone knew Eddie was married, frequently his girlfriends picked him up from the job site after work. Miraculously, his girlfriends never bumped into each other.

Eddie was so vain that he proudly told the story of how he and his son picked up a couple of hot numbers one night and took them to the same hotel room. I pity the woman who marries any of Eddie's sons as little as his sons have been taught to value their mother. Their skirt-chasing father has taught them the art of skirt-chasing well.

Whenever Eddie walked into a room in which I was standing and started his storytelling, I would walk out. Because there were so few blacks on the job and accusations of racism often charged the air like the high voltage electricity with which we frequently worked, most of the white men on the job could not understand why I did not like an affable, good-natured, humorous character like Eddie, who by the way, was an excellent electrician. Even though Eddie knew that I could not stand him, the moment he saw me he would walk up to me and tell me how nice I looked, as if a grimy construction worker could look nice. He would stand right in my face, well aware that he was invading my private space. His obsequious fawning and flattery annoyed me to no end and I frequently asked him to stop. The work crew thought that Eddie's persistence, in spite of my obvious disdain for him, was funny.

On the morning that I cursed Eddie out, the crew was assembling for general instructions before work. I was early so I sat there reading a newspaper. When Eddie entered the room, he did his usual act of pretending not to see anyone in the room but me. He walked over to where I was sitting and stood directly in my face, which was buried in the newspaper. I knew that Eddie was standing in front of me without looking up because I could hear the crew snickering. And so, I continued to read, ignoring Eddie. He continued to stand there for several minutes until finally I looked over the top of the newspaper. The crew was hysterical and I was furious. This was a daily game with Eddie.

As soon as we made eye contact, Eddie proceeded to tell me how lovely I looked and to say that he just wanted to say good morning. He continued to stand in my face flashing his usual stupid shit-eating grin. My anger was no longer controllable as I had tired of Eddie and his daily shows. Dropping all civil pretenses, I cut Eddie off before he could start his sycophant routine. I told him to get the fuck out of my face and cursed until I ran out of words. The words bounced off Eddie's thick skull like water off a duck's back. He laughed and commented that he had never seen me so "excited" before and told that me my excitement was very becoming. The electrician seated next to me handed me a pair of Klein's (a heavy metal plier designed for wire-cutting but frequently misused by electricians as a hammer because of its weight) and said, "Here, you'd better use these because this guy's head is thick!"

By now, the crew was rolling in the aisles and I was so angry my hands were shaking. I had made it clear to Eddie that I wanted no part of his foolishness but to him my feelings were irrelevant. He was intent on entertaining himself and the crew at my expense. I declined the pliers but my foreman, who normally laughed at Eddie's antics, shouted that everyone should get to work. The foreman, for whom I had worked previously and who had never heard me utter a single profanity, subsequently told Eddie to leave me alone because he did not want any trouble on the job. Only then did Eddie back off.

The brothers knew why I did not like Eddie, but they too anxiously awaited his arrival every morning to hear the story of his latest tryst that was always x-rated, explicit and very demeaning to some poor black woman, usually the woman picking him up from work that day. Often times the leering crew was peeping out the door when one of Eddie's women about whom they had heard a salacious story arrived to pick Eddie up. After all, the brothers lamented, Eddie was funny and the crew was just having fun.

To Eddie, women were just objects for his pleasure and amusement. He has taught his sons the same lesson. Though Eddie qualifies as a "provider" even under middle-class standards and may thus claim the title of patriarch, he is no solution to the problems facing black women. He is instead a very large part of the problem. Many of the white electricians from Long Island took Eddie's stories back to their all-white communities. These stories will be repeated for a long time to the detriment of any black women who will be sized up by these white males. My experiences have shown me that sexist beliefs about black women are not limited to the white community. Ignorance is the root cause of these myths in both communities. Books like the *Black Man's Guide* only fan the flame.

Much as Freud stressed penis envy in his analysis of the female species, the *Black Man's Guide* stresses that black women are jealous of black men because black men are capable of loving two different women at the same time, while black women are incapable of loving two different men at the same time. "They [women] are not equipped to handle two husbands, two sets of children, two households, two full responsibilities or two lifestyles."[47] However, a black woman could probably easily be a woman to two men at the same time if both men would assume total caretaker responsibility for the offspring produced and run both households much as most women presently do.

Additionally, the woman with two lovers would not be handicapped by the limitation of one erection a day. Thus even if she could not satisfy both lovers mentally and spiritually at all times, she could at least satisfy both sexually without having to resort to a juggling act. No doubt both men of the lover-girl wife, in spite of being sexually satisfied, would be as dissatisfied as most women today with lover-boy husbands. This is because love is not a question of sex and paying bills as those who confuse sex with love assume. Though someone has to keep a roof over the family's head, love is also a question of trust, utmost caring and intimacy.

In my short forty years on this earth, I have never seen love juggled successfully. I have, however, seen one relationship after another destroyed by lack of trust. Once trust is destroyed, the relationship is always more negative than positive. The juggler deludes only himself until his "act" comes crashing to his feet.

It simply is not true that most black women who find that their husbands are interested in other women will not give their husbands "another moment of peace until he has convinced her beyond all doubt that he has either changed his mind or wasn't serious about it in the first place."[48] Rather than spend a lifetime of suspicion and argument, many black women who are capable of surviving independently of their husbands simply leave or end the relationship. Thus the divorce rate continues to spiral. Those women who are kept "barefoot and pregnant" are seldom able to leave as their husbands are well aware. However, keeping these women prisoners in their own homes is not a solution to the problem of infidelity.

Some black women choose not to spend a lifetime in a relationship with men that they no longer trust, thereby giving these black men total freedom to pursue other women. And yet these men still complain. No doubt their complaint is that they cannot have their cake and eat it, too.

While I do not agree with the statement that, "There is no history of the black man settling down with one black woman and never desiring to have another,"[49] surely any man who purports to satisfy numerous women should not deny those women who are not satisfied with what he has to offer the right to leave. A relationship where one party is not free to leave is slavery. Slavery is more a question of whether one may exercise free will than whether one is forced to perform drudge work.

Thomas Jefferson is alleged to have bought his slave daughters the same dresses he bought his "legitimate" daughters, but his black daughters were slaves nonetheless, no matter how well they were treated in their white father's eyes. Jefferson's black daughters' condition of servitude precluded their exercise of free will. Therefore, unless we are willing to go back to slavery, where one class of persons was denied the opportunity to exercise free will, then that a man desires another woman but still wants his wife is not the deciding factor in whether his wife should choose to stay in the relationship or opt out. The wife may and should chose the option that is most satisfying for her needs, just as her husband seeks what he considers best for him.

No doubt there are some black women who are not bothered by how many women their husbands have as long as the husband brings home the check. If this particular group of women is not to the black man's liking, perhaps it is he who should change his standard as to the qualities he desires in a mate so that he will be more in tune with the pool of women that is available to him. For the black man to change his standards to accommodate the women who are agreeable to the "provider-womanizer" set-up is more sensible than trying to change those black women who want no part of this set-up. For the black male who has no intent of being faithful to his wife to consider a black female who chooses to remain faithful more desirable than the black female who does not choose to remain faithful is sexist hypocrisy. Those men who choose to play the field should hook up with women with a similar desire.

There is no need for any black man to lie "because he knows [the black woman] can't handle the truth about the reality of his life...."[50] Men who reject monogamy or one-on-one relationships should have the balls to state their position before entering a one-on-one relationship. They could thereby save themselves endless grief by giving those women who are totally opposed to man-sharing a chance to walk away before the relationship gets started. The man who chooses to lie and deceive a woman because he does not have the balls to stand up for his beliefs should not be surprised when a woman, who would never have gotten involved with him in the first place if she had known his true beliefs, is outraged on discovering his deceit. By deceiving his wife into thinking that he is something he is not, he has denied her the opportunity to choose a mate with beliefs more compatible with her own.

In spite of the propaganda in the *Black Man's Guide*, there are many black men who believe in monogamy. I know many professional young black men who are proud of their families, love their wives, and have no intent to fool around to satisfy pure ego or vanity. When I see a black man bring his baby to the classroom or bring his children to the office on Saturday when he is working overtime so that his wife may have a break, I see a man who I know loves his family. I have far more respect for this brother than I do for the brother who concerns himself only with the appearance of being the boss and keeping his wife and their children in their places.

I applaud the men, both black and white, who are making demands on their employers to accommodate their children. When I worked as an electrician in the computer rooms at Merrill Lynch, I loved to work on the Saturdays when the children of Merrill's employees were allowed to spend the day with their working parent. One could always tell the parents who were truly concerned about their children's well being. Many of the children were more impressive than their well-educated and affluent parents.

One would think that those men who intend to play around would content themselves with mates of a similar mentality, but strangely, those who want to play the field want mates who will be loyal. This is pure sexist hypocrisy. Once again, there are women who have no objection to their husband's womanizing as long as he brings home the check. The womanizers should content themselves with these women rather than attempt to deceive those women who want no part of such a scheme.

Just as men have the right to pursue their interests, women have the right to pursue women's interests. Just as men have peeves that they will not tolerate, women have peeves that they will not tolerate. The deceitful make life miserable for those who are honest and those who trust their significant others to reciprocate with honesty.

As a black woman, there are some things in life on which I will not compromise. Because these things go to the core of my value system, I do not attempt to hide them. Because of my strong feelings about these beliefs, I choose not to be involved with those who do not share these beliefs, be they black or white. Kinship requires more than skin color. I cannot tolerate racism, sexism, homophobia, drug addiction, incest, deliberate mistreatment of others, or womanizing. Because I respect the right of others to disagree with me, I wear my beliefs on my shirt sleeve for all to see. Those who cannot tolerate my philosophy need never waste their time fooling with me nor feel that I deceived them and thereby wasted their time.

"European rules and expectations of marriage"[51] have little to do with what I value in a relationship. I value what my eyes and heart have shown me is good. The few relationships that I have seen where the family worked together to get where it was going, rather than depend upon artificial role distinctions (where a family of able-bodied people will sit and go hungry rather than fix their own dinner or complain that they do not have clean clothes while the washer and dryer sit in the laundry room or there is a laundromat around the corner) have been so many light years ahead of the typical traditional family relationship that I would rather spend my life alone than perpetuate bullshit relationships merely for the sake of having a warm body in the bed next to me at night.

Sharing a bed with another warm body is not worth the price of my self-esteem. Those who find self-esteem in what I characterize as bullshit relationships should continue to enter these relationships, as is their right, but they need not seek to limit the experiences of other women to a similar mediocrity. Those women who believe that men have the right to slap them in the mouth, as is suggested by the *Black Man's Guide*,[52] need not encourage men to slap other women in the mouth as many women will not tolerate physical abuse. Some women do not want a man at all costs. This is not to put men down but to grant women the free will accorded to all adult citizens.

I, for one, choose not to perpetuate the oppression of women merely for the sake of companionship. I have tried to explain my beliefs to my son and I hope that he understands. I would be sorely disappointed to watch him marry a wife and then proceed to abuse her. I think that he will be kind and fair to the woman he marries someday and that makes me happy.

When my son was pre-school age, he frequently spoke of what we would do together when he grew up. I would tell him that when he grew up he would marry and could no longer live with me. He always protested. First, he would say that he would not get married. This always made me laugh because I knew that wild horses could not stop him from getting married once he made up his mind. I would tell him that he still could not live with me when he was grown because a grown man should have his own home. Then he would say that he would buy the house next door so that he could come over every day and that if I tried to run away he would call the police and have me brought back home. I found this hilarious. When I told him that he would be the one running away from me, he would shake his head, sit in my lap and hug me. He has long since passed the innocent stage of puppyhood and I suspect has grown weary of my endless rules and demands, but he has yet to run away. Each year I push harder in the hopes that one day he will discover that he can fly without me. I will miss him when he flies away but I am anxious to see him fly and train his own birds. Though my son is only fifteen, I at age forty, realize that each passing decade brings the reality of grandchildren closer.

Being forty myself, I read with some interest the comments in the *Black Man's Guide* about older black women (ages thirty-nine to fifty). Once again, the experiences presented were not my own. Though many young women (and men both black and white) have discussed problems related to their loved ones with me, not so much to get my advice as to find a sympathetic ear, I have never tried to turn a single person against marriage because of my failed marriage. I am not "full of stories of failed romances"[53] because since my divorce, I have been involved in only one serious relationship. I and the numerous black women in a similar position can hardly poison the minds of young women against black men because we have little to tell except that there are few black men available.

I was pleased as punch when a young couple whose first date I engineered three years ago got married this past spring, so much so that I cut my spring-break vacation short to attend their wedding. My only regret was that Erik did not finish law school like his lovely bride. Nonetheless, he is a good businessman and will succeed at any endeavor. Just yesterday I received a wedding invitation from another young, black female law student whom I encouraged to get married. I happily look forward to attending her wedding.

Contrary to what I read in the *Black Man's Guide*, most of the older black women who have counseled me against marriage have been black women who were themselves married. Other than my mother, my biggest booster in life was an old woman who was black as coal named Ma Prince. When I lived in the Midwest, she was like a mother to me. She had been married to the same man, Daddy Bully, for over fifty years. Daddy Bully was one of the few black men that I have known to marry a woman darker than himself. He married a treasure with skin of black velvet and with a heart more fecund than the deepest gold mines of Africa. I loved Daddy Bully almost as much as I love Ma Prince. Ma Prince always encouraged me to put my education first. After Ma Prince's death, I learned from her daughter that Ma Prince, who was dependent on social security, had saved the money I had sent her from New York to buy new dresses for herself just in case something happened to me that would cause me to need the money. I sent her money on occasion because she was so frugal that if the price were too high, she no longer liked the dress at which she had smiled the moment before. Her grandchildren knew that they could always get a dollar from Ma Prince because Ma Prince always had a dollar. She could stretch a dollar like a magician.

Ma Prince never stopped thinking of others. She took to my son as if he were one of her grandchildren. If, as the *Black Man's Guide* suggests, black men do not take in other black men like black women take in other black women, it is a pity and black men should do something to correct this grave error.[54] Though I have not lived around my blood relatives since graduating from high school, I have been lucky to find a few black families who took me in as their own. I have learned much from the black women who have taken me under their wings. I learned little of the foolishness presented in the *Black Man's Guide*.

When I was thirty years old, Ma Prince, who could talk anybody into anything, talked me into eating my first chitterlings. I had always considered myself too sophisticated to eat those smelly things. Ma Prince could cook tar paper and make it taste good. At her family reunions, she would put her arm around me and introduce me as her other daughter. Her husband, Daddy Bully, was the first man to take me hunting. On our first trip, he shot a rabbit and told me to tell Ma Prince that I had shot it. Though she would not dream of hunting an animal, when Ma Prince took the rabbit out of the bag, she laughed, clapped her hands and shouted with joy at the thought that I had learned how to handle a gun and could stalk prey in the frozen woods. Daddy Bully just winked at me.

Though both Ma Prince and Daddy Bully were more than forty years older than I, they never tried to keep me in a woman's place. Both used to tell me, "You do what you want to do! That's all that counts." I spent many pleasant weekends in their home. On Sunday nights, I hated to leave them. After my divorce when I was struggling to pay bills, maintain a home, finish my apprenticeship and find time for my preschool-age son, I was often so overwhelmed that I did not think I could go on. When I was so depressed that I thought I could not face another day, Ma Prince gave me strength and encouragement.

Other older black women that I have known have also encouraged me to put my education before the pursuit of a man. Another older black woman of whom I was quite fond, Thelma, used to tell me, "You just keep your nose in those books and you will do just fine." I used to delight in trying to distinguish between Thelma and her identical twin sister. I never learned to tell them apart. Everything about them was alike, including their freckles and the number of children each had.

At the time I was serving my apprenticeship with the electricians' union, I frequently visited Thelma. Her pipe-smoking husband, George, who was amazed that I had the nerve to challenge the lily-white union, would often break into my conversations with Thelma to tell me, "A black person serving an apprenticeship is unheard of in this town, but you keep it up. Yes, sir, you keep it up. It's a marvelous thing."

The older blacks in the community were my biggest supporters in spite of the fact that they had grown up in a different era with rigidly defined racial and sex roles. On Sundays and holidays, my son and I always had more invitations to dinner than we could accept.

I was as perplexed by the support I received from the older blacks in the community who had grown up with rigidly defined sex roles as I was by the statistics relating to married women and single women. Strangely, married men live longer than single men but single women live longer than married women. Though the *Black Man's Guide* tells us that an elderly black woman looks better if she has a man, the statistics do not bear this out. Marriage takes a toll on all women. Perhaps this is what my elderly friends were trying to tell me. Sometimes a woman has to make a choice between career and marriage. Both are not always compatible.

Although society is quick to acknowledge the disadvantages of women's biology, especially if a woman enters a non-traditional field, society is loathe to admit the advantages of women's biology or to suggest that we should accommodate these differences because of the resulting benefits to society. We generally sidestep the fact that society is quite dependent upon women choosing to exercise their procreational ability. Instead, women are told that we must play the game invented by men, for men, like men or not at all. For some reason, we are told that the male norm is better.

The shortsightedness of arguing which is better, male or female, may be illustrated by a simple hypothetical. Assume under the worst-case scenario of which the military is so fond, that there is nuclear armageddon resulting in only one man being left on the planet earth. Further assume that this man in his dutiful efforts to replenish the earth has intercourse 365 days a year. If his timing were just right, conceivably this lone man could impregnate 365 women in the course of one year and within nine months the births would commence. Consider also that if a sperm bank had been preserved within the ruins, the women could impregnate themselves without a single man being alive and the problem of inbreeding would be avoided in that conceivably each child could have a different father.

On the other hand, if after a catastrophic war only one woman were left on earth and 365 men, and the one woman had intercourse 365 days a year, only one birth could occur within a one-year time frame. The sexual activity would be virtually fruitless because in spite of the abundance of men, one woman can produce only one child within a nine month time frame, ignoring the time it takes for conception.

This brutal apprisal is not to put men down but instead to acknowledge the reality that from a purely biological, survival-of-the-species, worst-case scenario of which macho males are so fond, men are more expendable than women. Therefore, if one's concern is the survival of America, it makes more sense to ensure the preservation of females than males. This is why newspaper columns like Mr. William Raspberry's *To Restore the American Family, First Save the Boys* are fundamentally illogical and irrational. Logically, to preserve any race, it makes more sense to first save the females. Thus, it would have been more honest for Mr. Raspberry to say, to ensure the survival of the American system of male dominance, first save the boys. Survival and male dominance are two different issues, and it is illogical and irrational to confuse the two. From the male's perspective of entitlement, it is easy to confuse saving America with ensuring or preserving male dominance—just as from the white perspective of entitlement, it is easy to confuse saving civilization (or the neighborhood) with ensuring or preserving white dominance. However, survival and dominance are two separate issues.

This is not to say that women should be "preserved" in gilded cages. This is to say, however, that it makes perfect sense to allow those women who choose to fight for their country to assume combat positions while granting an exemption to those women who choose to exercise their procreational capacity. That men may not be granted this exemption is irrelevant in that men do not carry children inside their bodies as women do. Although we have gotten past the point where a women who wants out of her "place" is told that she must thereby learn to stand up and urinate like a man, we have not gotten much further. That every standard in life should be set by what men do or want to do is illogical.

It is also illogical to train women to be totally dependent upon men. If men perish, or simply change their affections, the women who are dependent upon men will also perish. The human species will die out with the death of the last woman, not the last man. 365 births per year versus 1 birth per year is a real difference that should be taken into account in planning the ultimate survival of the human race and the routine distribution of goods and services.

Perhaps instead of making plans to save the President of the United States and a bunch of aged male politicians when the button is pushed, we should concentrate on saving those women who are carrying children, or those women who have proved themselves capable of bearing children and who are capable of physically running and operating a sperm bank. Until test tube babies are perfected, men are simply more expendable than women. No doubt this is part of why we continue to spend billions of dollars a year on test tube baby technology while millions of babies already in existence languish and millions of adults already in existence either starve to death or die of dreadful diseases. The test tube baby technology is not being developed solely for the benefit of infertile women.

When babies can grow in test tubes or vats and women are no longer needed for the birthing process, it will be interesting to see whether the lot of women improves or deteriorates. I suspect it will deteriorate because I have never believed in the myth of male benevolence toward women. Opening the office door for a woman while at the same time stabbing her in the back in the game of office politics is not "benevolence" of any sort. Nor is placing one woman on a pedestal while condemning another to slave quarters or a ghetto even faintly benevolent. Ours is a system of male dominance and of keeping women off their guards while perpetuating a system of the oppression of women that has operated to the detriment of women for thousands of years.

It would be strange to discuss myths about black female sexuality without addressing homosexuality because the sexual experience of black women in America has not been limited to heterosexuality. I never particularly thought about the position of gays until about five years ago, shortly after I was battered and raped on a job site in New York City. Several months after the rape, when I tried to explain my feelings to a heterosexual black male who was a long-standing friend of mine, I was surprised by a comment that he made. Though we lived in different states, we generally kept in touch by phone and frequently discussed black male-black female relationships, often rather heatedly since we seldom agreed.

In one particular phone conversation, when I tried to explain to my friend something that had happened the day I was taken to the hospital that particularly disturbed me, a comment that he made started me to thinking about the real differences between males and females other than their sex organs. The police officer who accompanied me to the hospital was a white female. After she stayed with me as long as she could, she explained that she had to go back to work, said good-bye, and kissed me. In my panic stricken state, I had to stop myself from grabbing her shirt and crying, "Don't go!"

What stopped me from grabbing her and begging her not to go after she kissed me was the thought that she might view such reaction as a homosexual gesture and take offense. On the one hand it struck me as ludicrous to worry about being mistaken for a homosexual in my then distressing predicament. I was lucky to be alive. On the other hand I could not ignore the thoughts ricocheting like bullets inside my throbbing skull. The flashes of light from the ricocheting bullets were blinding, even though I knew that the sparks were inside my skull trying to get out, not outside my head trying to get in. I was too tired to think about it and so I did not. Instead I lay back and let the bright lights and voices continue to whir past in the vacuum of the emergency room. The woman in the bed next to mine was hemorrhaging and if I dared to look down from my spinning perch, I could see huge crimson splotches of blood on the white shoes of the white doctors in white coats that attended her. The day was one of madness.

Months later, I was still disturbed by the thoughts that raced through my head that day at the hospital. When I tried to explain to my male friend how annoyed I felt at having to deal with sex and the confusion that society places in our heads regarding sex, he said that he could understand why some women turned away from men just to avoid the hassles of dealing with sex. He told me that his ex-wife had been raped some ten years earlier and that their relationship had never been the same afterwards. I was shocked when he said, "I can understand how a woman who turns away from men could love another woman because women are basically kind, loving and nurturing, soft and warm, gentle and supportive, but I could never understand how two dudes could love each other because men are basically cold and self-centered."

On a superficial level, I had always thought that men were somehow different from women, but I had never examined those differences more than superficially. During the phone conversation, it occurred to me then that at a much deeper level, being a woman is more than a physical condition but is instead a mental state. Normally the mental state that goes along with being a woman is associated with physically being a woman, but why should this be so? The few homosexual men that I have known have generally been more warm, open and caring than the traditional heterosexual male. I do not know whether this is because they have come to understand oppression better than other males or because by nature they are more sensitive than other males. I do know that the few homosexual women that I have known have been as warm and caring as heterosexual women, only for some reason they prefer intimate relationships with other women. Because I do not see being nurturing or warm and caring as negative traits, I cannot condemn the homosexual men or women who value these traits and seek them in a same-sex partner.

Though I cannot imagine being physically in love with another woman, who am I to place the limits of my vision on another human being? Even when I was only eight years old, I hated it when others sought to impose the limits in their minds upon me, whether it was my father telling me to go back into the house with my mother before I turned into a tomboy, or the new white librarian at the bookmobile telling me that there was no way I could read twelve books in two weeks time when I knew (as did the previous librarian who not only let me take extra books but often saved them for me) that I would read the books in one week's time and then read some of the books my older sister checked out. Having grown accustomed to the limits others have always sought to place on me, I am not so anxious to do the same to others.

The hostility directed against black lesbians by the *Black Man's Guide* was extraordinary. One would think that those women who are consumed with catching and keeping a black male would rejoice in the fact that the more lesbians there are who do not compete for the attention of males, the more black men that will remain available for everyone else. As difficult as I have found life to be for those like me who are black and female, I cannot imagine that any black woman, as the *Black Man's Guide* suggests, would take on the additional handicap of being lesbian simply to endear herself to the feminist movement. The feminist movement all too often excludes the experiences of black women and often appears embarrassed by its "dykes." I do not refer to lesbianism as a handicap to be insulting to lesbians but instead to reflect my experience that being "different" in any substantial way is a handicap. There were enough insults to black lesbians in the *Black Man's Guide* that I need not add fuel to the flame. If I do so in ignorance, I offer my apology.

The myths presented in the *Black Man's Guide* about lesbians were absurd. The notion of the monolithic homosexual experience is as

115

mythical as the monolithic heterosexual experience. All homosexuals do not look alike or act alike anymore than all heterosexuals or blacks look and act alike. Homosexuals are no more likely to molest children or engage in criminal sexual activity than heterosexuals.

Being a lesbian has absolutely nothing to do with an "idea based on the belief that she knows how to treat a black woman better than the black man."[55] Homosexuality is a preference for the same sex, not a hatred of the opposite sex. Lesbians are merely women who are attracted to those of the same sex as themselves. This is not to say that they hate men. Why should lesbians hate men anymore than homosexual men hate women, or heterosexual men hate other men, or heterosexual women hate other women? Why is it that we cannot sit down and think about these things rationally and logically instead of responding to our training to bash anything that is different?

The notion that a lesbian "becomes violent if provoked"[56] is as perverse as the notion that all blacks are violent or that all blacks steal. The notion that "she [the lesbian] overdoes it and makes herself a spectacle that is not welcome among civilized people,"[57] is equally as absurd. Those not welcome "among civilized people" have traditionally included all people of color. That lesbians should also be lumped into the uncivilized category is not surprising. What is surprising is that blacks, of all people, could believe that all lesbians or all homosexuals look or act a certain way. Most of us walk past homosexuals every day without knowing who they are.

When my ex-husband was at the height of his athletic career and stood about six feet, three inches and weighed about 260 pounds, he mentioned to me that he had been approached by homosexual males at private athletic clubs whom no one would ever believe were homosexual because of their similar muscular appearance. There is no monolithic homosexual profile anymore than there is a monolithic black profile or female profile. People are whatever they are.

The Black Man's Guide ignorantly confuses lesbians with transsexuals. Women who "wear men's clothes, talk like [men], take steroids or hormones to resemble [men] and develop other masculine traits,"[58] are transsexuals, not lesbians. If we are going to apply labels, should not we get the labels straight? I for one would like to know what the "lesbian black woman repelled by the secret normal looking black woman who practices lesbianism,"[59] looks like. I fear that in my short forty years on this earth, I have managed to miss seeing this awesome creature but I cannot understand how. I would also like to know what the "normal looking" black woman looks like. Does she look like Jayne Kennedy? Vanessa Williams? Tina Turner? Lonette McKee? Janet Jackson? If so, then many dark-skinned, thick-lipped black women with broad noses are not "normal" looking. Perhaps this is why some wealthy black women have plastic surgery, so that they can look "normal."

This is not to put down white-looking black women, but instead to acknowledge the suspectness of a beauty standard whereby white-looking black women are consistently rated as more attractive than African-looking black females by those who claim to be black and proud. I find such a selection process as suspect as the selection process whereby white employers who claim to be equal opportunity employers remarkably hire only white employees.

In a world where many women's hair is naturally short, to say that dykes cut their hair short is to say nothing meaningful and does not give us a clue as to who these women are, what they look like, or why we should be alarmed at their presence among us. It is not the homosexuals that I fear lurking in the bushes when I leave the law library at midnight or when I park my car in my deserted garage. No homosexual has ever done anything to me except perhaps to question my value system.

Though professing to tell us all about lesbians, the *Black Man's Guide* failed to make a distinction between homosexuals and homosexual activity. Many men and women confined to a single sex environment, e.g., prison, will resort to homosexual activity until removed from the environment. Is this to say that these men and women are homosexuals? If so, then probably many of us are homosexuals. I find it difficult to believe that the men and women who engage in homosexual activity while confined to a single-sex environment are homosexuals because once released from confinement, many return exclusively to heterosexual activity. While I do not profess to understand the difference between homosexuality and homosexual activity or whether the difference is even relevant, I am not prepared to dismiss the homosexual experience as an aberration simply because I do not understand it. All my life whites and black men have dismissed my experiences as a black woman as irrelevant because they have failed to understand my experiences. How quickly the oppressed become the oppressor when even the black woman presumes to dismiss the experiences of another black woman without even attempting to examine or understand that experience.

Truly all of us are blinded by our prejudices in spite of the innocence we profess. Whatever the system of discrimination that is implemented, once implemented it perpetuates itself. No master-mind or blue-eyed devil is required to maintain any system of discrimination because ignorance, like bacteria and disease, continually perpetuates itself.

Chapter 8

The Resolution of Problems in the Black Community

Black women must no longer allow their history to be distorted by whites or black men. Black women must no longer allow themselves to be oppressed by whites or black men. Black women must deal with all who oppress us if our condition is ever to improve substantially. If dealing with our oppression means that we will be labeled the divisive Sapphire by those who continue to reap the benefits of our oppression, so be it. We can no longer afford to run from our battle or sit idly, praying and waiting. In light of four hundred years of history, we have no choice except to deal with the people and systems who oppress us.

One of those oppressors has been the black male. Much as whites who "sympathize" with blacks sit silently while blacks are denied jobs and housing and are spurned socially, many black men sit silently while black women are mentally and physically abused, denied opportunities for advancement and spurned socially. Sexism, like racism, is easily perpetuated as even those who call themselves sympathetic are loathe to challenge a racist or sexist friend about his or her statements and beliefs about blacks or women. Sexists, like racists, are thereby free to continue their hateful discrimination unchecked. They are not perceived as dangerous to their friends and family as long as they threaten only those outside their social circle. Meanwhile, blacks and women catch hell. The mistreatment of black males by white society is just as unjust as the mistreatment of black women by white society and black males.

Both types of mistreatment allow the undeserving to reap economic and social benefits by turning their backs to the denial of access to others. Both allow the perpetrators to thereby enjoy privileges and perquisites that should never have accrued to them in the first place. Both allow the perpetrators to claim they are entitled to access that they never obtained fairly in the first place, and would never have obtained but for the denial of access to others long ago. Both allow the perpetrators to claim that they are the most qualified and that others should now prove themselves worthy, of course, long *after* the rules regarding access have been changed from entitlement to merit. Both allow the current perpetrators who reap the benefits of the system to claim innocence. Both deny the reality of the racial and sexual politics that have reigned from day one and the reality of the present conditions that have resulted from the politics of double standards. Both are pure hypocrisy.

In spite of the black woman's touted strength and advantage at being a double minority, we are still at the bottom rung of the ladder of life. Something is clearly wrong. We can start to remedy our oppression by eliminating the double standards that exist in our communities, especially those that exist in our own homes where our children receive their first lessons in life.

The first lesson in life for black girls is how little they are valued even in their own communities. Not only do they watch how the double standards of the marketplace and marriage affect their mothers, but also young girls learn that even in the realm of entertainment when the chores of work and family are put aside, black women still are not worth anything. In their own homes and on every street corner, black girls hear rap music sung by black men touting the virtues of sexual violence against women. All this is done in the name of free speech and the black man's right to express himself like the white man. Take for example the lyrics of 2 Live Crew:

> *To have her walkin' funny we try to abuse it*
> *A big stinking pussy can't do it all*
> *So we try real hard just to bust the walls*

Young girls constantly bombarded with the same message over and over, quickly come to understand that the walls are vaginal walls and that to bust the walls means to bust the walls of women's vaginas—women who are almost always called bitches or "hoes," women who are forced to perform anal sex or lick feces. Because black men have the right to express themselves, black women are bombarded with lyrics such as:

> *He'll tear the pussy open 'cause it's satisfaction.*
> *Suck my dick, bitch, it makes you puke.*[60]

> *I'm the nigger you love to hate bitch. Back off my*
> *tip because 'cause you on it like a gnat on a dog's dick.*[61]

We can talk about free speech forever, and we can rave at the unfairness of limiting free speech after black men discover a way to capitalize off free speech much like the white man and his pornography and other forms of tasteless entertainment. Many whites will support the black man's right to this free speech because clearly, the women being sung about are black women, not white women. As history has shown, whenever black men are perceived a threat to white women, the entire white community will rise to the white woman's defense. If the Central Park jogger who was brutalized and raped had been black, her assailants could well be walking the streets today.

Though eventually the lyrics of explicit sexual violence against women (oral obscenity), like the crack phenomenon, may rear its ugly head on a mass scale in the white community, for the moment, it is black women who must walk the streets in the black communities where this kind of misogyny and sexual violence against black women is glorified by a boom box on every corner and endless cranked up car radios. It is black women who must confront white men in every direction in which we turn—white men who for centuries have had a license to rape black women, and who now long after the emancipation hear black men singing about the glory of bustin' black pussies. It is the images of the niggah bitches and "hoes" of the black man, i.e., the black man's women, that come to mind when one listens to (or views videos) black rappers sing about "bustin' pussies," not the images of the kinder gentler white woman who is still considered the exclusive property of the white man. The black men who live in her world do not sing about bustin' her pussy. Instead she is treasured like gold.

These lyrics are not mere off-color nursery rhymes that turn the stereotypes of black and white American culture on their heads as some who make excuses for the rappers suggest.[62] In fact these images are not even new. The hostility of dick-grabbing black comedians like Eddie Murphy towards black women has, like the volume, merely been pumped up. Now instead of bustin' Sapphire upside the head, black men are bustin' Sapphire's pussy. It did not take much imagination. One had only to look down. It is the same old game, only nastier.

Once again the black woman is told she should praise the genius of the black men who continually capitalize off of her by insulting her. This time the genius is called rap instead of comedy. The black woman who dares to criticize rap is given the kiss of death. After all, the brothers must be allowed to assert themselves, to be black men in the cruel white man's world. No thought is ever given to what it is like to be a black woman in not only the cruel world of white men but also the cruel world of black men.

Time will tell whether the black rappers, like the dick-grabbing black comedians who have grown rich telling us about the problem with Sapphire, will also have a penchant for white wives in spite of their ongoing love affair with Sapphire. Dare these "pioneering" brothers rap about their white ladies? The black comedians certainly do not tell raunchy jokes about their white women. The young generation of rappers seem to be following in the footsteps of the old brothers who have by now managed to boost themselves into other industries, most particularly the motion picture industry. Unlike the threat these brothers pose to black women, they are no threat to white women because the system will protect white women even if only after the fact.

The rappers should warn the brothers that the black men who attempt to bust white pussies will meet the fate of the black men who attempt to bust their white wives in the mouth. But then again, most brothers probably already know. Though the *Black Man's Guide* tells us that Sapphire deserves to have her head busted when she does not behave, lord help the brother who is so confused as to attempt to bust the head of a white woman, even if she is his wife. Even the mighty Juice, California's sweetheart O. J. Simpson, found himself in the custody of L.A.P.D. when he dared to raise a hand to his white wife. Luckily for O.J., the L.A.P.D. crew that arrested him was not the same crew that arrested poor Rodney King.

It will be interesting to see if the black rappers who bombard the nameless children in the black community with their "music" will bombard their own young offspring with the same lyrics. No doubt the rappers' children will go to schools in nice suburban communities where there are few blacks and few boom boxes broadcasting obscenities about anything even vaguely related to the problems in the black community.

I abhor rap lyrics because they contribute to the continued devaluation of black women. These lyrics contribute to the world's negative image of Sapphire: big butts, big thighs, big mouths, always ready, no foreplay required because these sisters are hot! As she has done since her childhood, Sapphire pops out babies just to collect a check. She just cannot help the fact that she was born to "hoe." It's in her blood. In spite of the many contributions black women have made to this country, the image of the contentious whorish Sapphire prevails over all other images of black women in both the black and white communities.

Black women have contributed much to this society in spite of the tremendous odds they faced as the "slaves of slaves." Though the black woman is often an embarrassment to white America and to the black man and is thus treated as if she were invisible, irrelevant or non-existent, the black woman is very much alive. The black woman must not be made a scapegoat by white society or the black man for problems she did not create and cannot solve of her own volition.

The history of black women in America goes much deeper than spending all of our time "scamming" on the black man and running him into the ground, as was backwardly suggested by the *Black Man's Guide*. Many of the successful black men that I know have been raised single-handedly by their working-class mothers. A good friend of mine with a Ph.D. in chemistry was raised by his mother's sister after the death of his mother, who had long been abandoned by his father. He does not appear particularly warped. Black women have been in the forefront of movements to improve their communities and the civil rights movement though we are loathe to admit the contributions of black women lest black men be made to appear weak.

It is outrageous for blacks to seek to hide our problems to make ourselves more palatable to racist whites. To waste even five minutes of our time pandering to the opinions of whites who cannot stand us anyway and will continue to look for excuses to run us into the ground in spite of what we do is lunacy. Racism is not rational. Neither is trying to hide the fact that the black race, like every other race, is only human and that blacks make mistakes and have problems, too. Just as the white race's denial of what happened to the native American Indians will not bring a single Indian back to life, our denial of the problems in the black community will not save a single black victim from suffering.

Such pandering behavior strangely resembles that of the battered wife caught in the steel grip of the battered wife syndrome. Surprisingly, battered wives who have been beaten close to death continue to bow down to and to try to appease the husbands who daily beat them senseless, much as blacks with a four hundred year history of abuse in America continue to try to mollify our persecutors who will never consider us "equal."

Though I have the greatest respect and admiration for Martin Luther King, Jr., I do not believe his dream that someday blacks will be judged by the content of their character rather than the color of their skin will ever come true. No society has ever existed where whites considered blacks as equals and no such society will ever exist. Blacks will continue to die waiting, hoping and praying.

Neither is it likely that a legal defense parallel to the battered wife syndrome, such as a battered black syndrome, will be implemented to save blacks from our own self-destructive behavior. As the conviction rate of black women who retaliate against their black abusers bears out, American juries have enough trouble believing that black women, like white women, may be victims of a battering syndrome. They are too well acquainted with the image of the bodacious black Sapphire. That an entire race of blacks could still be suffering from the lingering effects of slavery is incomprehensible from the white perpetrator perspective that is willing to acknowledge only individual violations of civil rights where the victim can point a finger at the perpetrator. Self-destructive blacks will continue to perish.

Because of their own sickness, the abusive husbands of battered women can never be appeased. The more the wife gives, whether love or submission, the more the insatiable husband will demand. Likewise, racists whites will never be satisfied with the appeasement offerings of blacks. Those blacks who nonetheless seek to play the game of appeasement should place the burden of appeasement on themselves instead of on black women.

There is no way to win the sick game of appeasement of the batterer until one of the players is permanently eliminated from the game. If blacks continue to play this game of physical and psychological torture with whites, a game that often leads a battered woman to take the life of her batterer, blacks may score a few victories as do some abused wives. However, in the long run no doubt it is blacks who will eventually be permanently taken out of the game on a stretcher. The odds are always in favor of the batterer.

We cannot continue to let the opinions of whites define who and what the black race is or should be because every time whites change the definition, blacks like chameleons must change to suit white expectations. Our energies will be consumed by pandering rather than improving our lot. With the odds that blacks face today, improving our lot will consume generations of blacks to come.

The black woman is not a magic talisman by whose possession the black man may gain or conjure up freedom or the world's respect or his own self-respect. Contrary to what the proponents of the matriarchy theory would have us believe, the black man's biggest problem is not the black woman but is instead the racist capitalist market created by whites, designed to serve the interests of dominant white males. If black women ceased to exist tomorrow, black men would continue to experience difficulties in a marketplace that is designed to promote the interest of dominant white males while nevertheless granting any man the right to dominate any woman so as to placate the non-dominant males and thereby garner their loyalty to the system.

Even so, this market is designed to promote the interests of males over females as is evidenced by the fact that in the market, all males, even black males, routinely outearn females, including white females. Thus the black female is far more disadvantaged than the black male. Economically and socially, it is the black female and her children who are at the bottom rung of the ladder of life.

The black community as well as the white community must drop the sexist assumption that the experiences of men are more important than the experiences of women and that what matters most in the male experience is that men are able to assert themselves patriarchally. Millions of black women, from doctors and lawyers to unemployed welfare mothers who have never had jobs, will continue to lead lives that are basically devoid of black men whether by choice or necessity. These women's experiences are just as important as the experiences of any black male. The notion that we need not concern ourselves with the life experiences of women who are not attached to men is sexist and absurd whether the proponent is a white male or a black male.

Such sexist notions operate to force women to attach themselves to men and to submit to abuse to survive in a world in which all too often women cannot support themselves. Some unfortunate women have even submitted to the sexual abuse of their daughters by their husbands or lovers just to keep a roof over the family's head. This sickness does not exist only in the white community.

The story of Carolivia Herron, now a professor at Mt. Holyoke and a fellow at Yale, is a story of horror. In her own words:

> Two or three times a week I was taken from nursery school to a house of prostitution...where I became the partner of a man called Big White Daddy.... [The first time] he lowered me onto him, I thought it was an accident, but instead of lifting me off, he just jumps on the bed with me. You can imagine the scream: I was 4 years old.[63]

The sicknesses of sexist oppression exist in the black community as well as in the white community. We are fooling no one by closing our eyes to the reality of the abuse of the black woman. We are, however, insuring the continued victimization of our daughters.

It is especially crucial that we take account of the experiences of the black women who, for whatever reason, are unable to provide for themselves and their children. Many of these women live in such poverty and despair that they can no longer wait for the black man or Jesus or Uncle Sam. Daily, they watch their children die. These women need immediate help in pulling themselves up, or their families will continue to perish. Their children simply cannot fend for themselves. The narcotic of dependency of which some warn us cannot be cured by shooting the children of those women who are dependent. Somehow these women must humanely be pulled out of dependency without destroying their children.

One of the saddest stories I have ever read was that of a young toddler who had been placed in the oven by his mother to exorcise the demons from his body. After he was burned almost to death and was taken from the custody of his mother, the nurses who attended him could not believe that he cried for his mother. When asked why he was so upset at being taken from the woman who almost killed him he responded sadly, "She's still my mother and I still love her."

Though many deny the bonding process or attachment of mothers to their children and vice-versa, society must be prepared to reckon with this factor if children with deficient mothers are to be helped. Whether mom is a dope addict, prostitute, or child abuser, her children still love her and want her and probably always will. Any remedy that denies this factor is short-sighted indeed, for the participation and cooperation of the children will be difficult to garner.

This is not to put men and their relationships with their children down. Instead, it is simply to admit that the relationship between a woman and the child that she has carried in her body for nine months is more than physical whether we care to admit it or not and whether it is fair to men or not. Much as men have the advantage of muscle mass, women have the advantage of an almost universal bonding process with the children they bear. Men who wish to bond with their children must generally work at what by birth comes naturally to most women. Men of all races have been heard to complain that "She loves that child more than she loves me."

In the years that I worked the electrical trade, an old Italian foreman I worked for used to counsel young newly married electricians who had recently become fathers and who complained of their wives' affection for the children that it was better that their wives should love the children more rather than to love another man more. He used to joke that he was glad his wife of forty years loved his children more than she loved him because he knew that the kids would never raise a hand to hurt her. Therefore, no matter how sternly he disciplined the kids, he knew that his wife could always stop the kids from killing him by physically standing in front of him. Though there is an exception to every rule, nature has ensured that most women will take care of their children.

Poor women have no monolithic experience by which they can be identified except their perceived ability to bear children. Whether they live in remote rural areas, metropolitan areas or inner-city ghettos, all suffer. The danger in limiting the black females' experience to that of the black female in the inner-city ghetto is that it makes it too easy for whites to conclude that where there is no ghetto in sight, there is no race problem. Meanwhile, black women and their children continue to suffer.

The black woman is in a curious predicament in that those who are not dependent and submissive are viewed as castrating bitches but those who are dependent and submissive have difficulty surviving in a world where large numbers of the black males on which these women depend are permanently disqualified from the marketplace by illiteracy and criminality, large numbers are handicapped by racism, and large numbers prefer white women or black women of a lighter complexion. In spite of the shortsightedness of some black women who prefer dependence, we cannot sit back and simply allow them to perish after we have trained them to be dependent. Something must be done about the condition of all women in America, especially the poor women who are the least able to fend for themselves.

Independent women pay a great price also in a society where they are viewed as castrating bitches. For too many black women—even the so-called successful—dogged disaster is always one step behind. Many of us have been running scared since our first brush with the fate that awaits the castoff and downtrodden. They perish daily. A decent burial is the most that far too many black women can hope for. Many of the black women who are survivors are never at peace. They are too well acquainted with the horrible specter that is always one step behind, sucking the very oxygen out of the air that they breathe. For these women, dark shadows are a way of life.

Tragically, many black women are labeled hard, cold or aloof because of their life experiences. Most black women do not live like the beautiful fairy princesses in the white community with daddies like kings and lovers like ambitious princes who would be kings, both of whom cater to the little princess's every need, as long as the little princess is content to remain in the gilded cage.

The bars on Sapphire's cage are hard, cold steel and often the cage is ringed with a barbed-wire fence lest the cunning Sapphire escape the first trap. Should she escape the snare of sexism, there is always the snare of racism, or vice-versa. Sapphire is well acquainted with the dark shadows that are constant reminders of the harsh and often cruel fate that awaits her with one careless misstep. There are no pedestals and few knights in shining armor for the sisters who are well acquainted with violence, tragedy, deprivation and oppression. For many black women, their children are their only joy in life. At one time a black women could be assured that her children would be with her at least until age eighteen, but with the crack-cocaine phenomenon even three-year-olds and babes in arms are being taken from their mothers. Tragically, after being carried to term, many newborns cannot survive their drug-addicted delivery.

For many black women who must support their children, work has always been a way of life because of the poverty that haunts their communities. Changing these black women into fairy princesses in black face is not a magic solution to the problems that deluge the black community, unless the wave of the magic wand can also change the skin color of all those in the community. Wherever there is discrimination there will be poverty and despair, whether in a big-city ghetto or a poor rural area. Oppression, like poverty and despair, does not need a ghetto to survive.

Though I was not raised in a ghetto, I, like most blacks have been much affected by oppression, poverty and despair. Oppression, poverty and despair follow those of us with dark skins like day follows night. The untimely deaths of a number of my relatives was a result of the conditions of oppression, poverty and despair that haunt blacks in America.

In spite of the fact that all my relatives were ordinary people living ordinary lives, all were struck by the extraordinary tragedy that haunts those with black faces.

My aunt and grandmother were murdered in a domestic dispute. My uncle Red was shot in the head during a robbery. My cousin Rita (Red's daughter) was found dead and decaying at a dump site with her hands tied behind her back, a plastic bag over her head and her mouth stuffed with rags on the seventeenth anniversary of her father's death. My ex-husband's deaf uncle Ronnie unknowingly walked into gunfire in a neighborhood dispute and was shot to death. Many years ago my ex-husband's uncle Skee Joe was shot to death in front of his three young children when he made the mistake of moving into an all-white neighborhood in Chicago that is now all-black. My kind, loving and gracious cousin Junior, who always made us laugh, who had a knack for talking his parents out of whipping him by making them laugh, and whom I had adored since childhood, was burned alive in an explosion at a Texas oil refinery. I cannot imagine the look of terror that must have been on his always smiling and gentle face. The company that was responsible for Junior's death paid dearly for its mistake, but as for my other deceased relatives, none of the perpetrators responsible for their deaths even said "I'm sorry" to the surviving families who had to pick up the pieces.

The law does not recognize the fear and anxiety I feel at these losses because the law is unwilling to recognize the harsh conditions under which blacks labor. We are not simply whites with black faces. We are a race that has been bastardized by white men and subjected to hundreds of years of institutionalized brutal oppression. Our history has been the worst of what life has to offer. Changing the law does not change history and the conditions that have resulted from that history. The tentacles of oppression continue to reach into the future and claim victims.

The law does not recognize that being born black in America is itself a hazard. Though in theory the law is blind to color, in reality the world is not blind to the color the courts refuse to see. Blacks are thereby condemned to a schizophrenic existence where we pretend to live in one world, but in reality we live in another. The dark-skinned who have been forced to adapt to the schizoid world of double standards well understand the agony of knowing that on any given day of the week, one is vulnerable to disaster because of skin color alone. The additional burden of being vulnerable because of one's sex can make life unbearable. Unfortunately, there is no place to hide.

The double standard that exists in many black homes between the standards imposed on male and female offspring is no different from the double standard that exists in America regarding the races. Both produce disastrous inconsistencies and result in endless confusion. A woman who learns not to accept second-class citizenship on account of her race is in a gut-wrenching double bind when she is told that she must accept second-class citizenship on account of her sex.

Because often there is no one to speak for black women besides black women, black women must continue to speak out about abuses in spite of being labelled as treacherous Sapphires. If we do not speak, who will? Our submission will not ensure that our abuse will end. All too often, our submission ensures only our continued abuse. The most likely victim cannot afford to remain silent. Black men have oppressed black women just as whites have. The myth of the black knight rescuing his feminine helpmate is dangerous in that many black women who are too dependent and submissive to support themselves have perished and continue to perish as ladies in waiting and also-rans.

Femininity is a trap for many women. In spite of what society tell us, femininity is not defined by the length of one's fingernails, hair, or skirt. All too often, femininity is defined by powerlessness. However, femininity is an inner quality which may be lacking in spite of superficial appearances just as masculinity may be lacking in spite of superficial appearances. Wearing pants does not make a man any more than wearing a skirt makes a woman.

Contrary to what the patriarchs and would-be patriarchs tell us, a chicken in every pot and a penis in every household is not the solution to the black community's problems. The solution to the black community's problems is men and women who can provide for their families and have respect for each other. Replication of the white community in black face is only a temporary solution and then only for those women who are labeled "desirable" by their male selectors.

The submission for protection rubric has begun to break down even in the white community. The large numbers of white women who protest daily provide ample testimony that the gilded cage might not be so great after all. Even the most privileged of white women are opting out. Whatever differences black women may have with white women, for black women to rush into the very cages that white women are trying to escape is of questionable wisdom, no matter how heavy the gilding or how extravagant the promises of the men holding the keys. The condition of all women will improve most when women can stand independently and select mates by choice, not necessity.

All too often, black men view sexism from the perpetrator perspective much as whites view racism from the perpetrator perspective. Just as the perpetrator perspective addresses racism from the standpoint of individual remedies, as opposed to addressing the condition of minorities, the perpetrator perspective addresses sexism from the viewpoint of individual remedies as opposed to addressing the condition of women. From this perspective, women who take their battles to the civil right arena will fare no better than blacks have in the civil rights arena. Sadly, sex discrimination like race discrimination is a social phenomenon, not just the result of the isolated acts of a few bad eggs. Discrimination is bad whether intentional or not and whether a particular cause or culprit may be identified or not. Much of sexism, like racism, is unconscious, therefore nearly impossible to address or eradicate. Therefore the victim *and* the perpetrator must cease to cling to old myths if the condition of women is to improve.

Mindlessly clinging to old myths is plain dangerous. Especially where conditions continue to deteriorate, myths must be challenged and examined. A solution that has not brought relief in the past four hundred years is not likely to bring relief in the next thousand years, and should be abandoned. Blacks, most especially black women, must use whatever control we have to change our conditions.

We must be especially diligent in working with our youths because they are our future. Our youths should be discouraged from automatically bringing up the rear. In light of the overwhelming problems that face our black youths, we should be particularly concerned with increasing the black judiciary since all too often the outcome of any case is determined by who sits on the bench. Our inner-city youths have unheralded problems that require unheralded dedication and commitment to change and that will also result in many of our youths landing in a court of law. The old ways will not save these troubled youths as at no time in history have the problems facing youths been so overwhelming and total disaster loomed so near.

A standing joke among many attorneys is that there is no law, only judges. For blacks, there is nothing funny about this joke. As The Honorable Justice Thurgood Marshall reminded us on tendering his resignation from the ultra-conservative Supreme Court, "It is not the law that has changed but the personnel on this Court."[64] The hands on the clock are going backwards in the midst of this our Second Reconstruction. After a lifetime of struggle, surely Justice Marshall deserves a refuge from the struggle. Though I have never met Justice Marshall, I love and respect him as a father. He is truly a magnificent man. However, we cannot afford to wait for another Thurgood Marshall to come along to save us. Men like Justice Marshall, be they black or white, come along only once in every thousand years.

Though men like Justice Marshall who have worked doggedly all of their days should have some rest, for the rest of black America, there is no time for rest or peace. Nor should there be any peace for white America until the problems of racism are eradicated. Racism, like sexism, is too easily swept under the rug by those who reap the advantages.

Therefore, the disadvantaged must use whatever resources are available to improve our conditions. We can no longer afford to wait or ignore conditions that continue to degenerate. We must become actively involved in every arena in which our problems may be addressed.

The sooner the black man and the black woman work through their problems, as opposed to brushing them under the rug, the sooner the black man and woman can move forward together, assuming they choose to move forward together. Many blacks have opted out on this choice as is their right. However, it is doubtful that the day will ever come when the races are so intermingled that everyone is the same color and racism disappears. As more blacks intermarry with whites, those whites who still look "white" or have a special claim to whiteness will probably be considered more elite because of their dwindling numbers.

Additionally, in a society of male dominance where the offspring of two-parent families take the father's name, assume the father's identity, move wherever the father's job necessitates, and generally live in the father's world, many black-skinned children of white fathers and black mothers (unlike their black-skinned counterparts of white mothers and black fathers) could well be labelled white in spite of their dark skin. Will the black community force these mixed children to pick a race? This would be a travesty because these children are not white or black. They are both.

One of the white male law professors whose class I enjoyed most is a white man who is married to a black woman. In class, he spoke frequently of his attorney wife and her courtroom experiences, but he never told us she was black. (Why should he?) The day after his son was born, he came to class after an all-night ordeal looking much like a refugee. The class gave him an ovation and insisted that he go home, but the proud papa was determined to teach. In spite of his fatigue, he was beaming.

When I watch him play with his young son, I see a loving father who could easily raise his son as father knows best, from his perspective as a white male. Can those who support male dominance and the theory that only a man can raise his son to be a man deny the white man the right to raise his dark-skinned sons as white males? Will we label the dark-skinned boys raised by white men who identify with their white fathers traitors to the black race?

After meeting this white professor's lovely black wife, I know that they will have no problem in raising well-adjusted children, but what about those mixed couples who are not so enlightened? If males should dominate the relationships with their sons, should the white male seek to dominate his black wife and raise his son as a white male? Just as

131

there is a difference in being biologically female (one's sex) and culturally female (one's gender), there is a difference in being biologically black (or white) and culturally black (or white). Just as one may be biologically male and culturally female (or vice-versa), one may appear biologically black and yet be culturally white (or vice-versa). Will the black community scorn the culturally white black-skinned male or female?

Black men and black women do not agree on everything. It would be quite unnatural if we agreed on everything. Many blacks define "success" as being like whites but many others do not. Instead of yearning for the good old days when men kept women in their place, or as some would suggest, when whites kept blacks in their place, our time might be better spent in trying actively to evolve some kind of new social order in which all may have a part, rather than letting an idea whose time has come develop like the patch-work quilt of integration that is good for decoration but has little warmth.

The old order has already irretrievably broken down. Some of us have no interest in going back. Some of us have no interest in going forward. And so, we continue to fight a war that no one can win. As has been true throughout history, our memories are short and already we have forgotten the Viet-Nam war, the war that no one could win. And so, the propaganda of patriarchy, neutrality and equality continues to fly and the victims in the black community continue to fall in record numbers. Body bags are a way of life in many communities where black bodies fall like the tree leaves in the Vietnamese forests that were sprayed with the defoliant agent orange.

Covering up the problems in the black community lest we be made to look bad in the white community is a senseless tactic. This tactic, like covering an infected sore, only allows the infection to fester and grow beneath the surface. It will take more than cosmetics to cure a sore that has a four hundred-year-old scab. It is about time that we remedy the conditions of racism and sexism instead of looking to short-term quick fixes in both the white and black communities.

Though I deplore books like the *Black Man's Guide* for their continued devaluation of the black woman, simple-minded myths, glib oversimplifications of facts that appeal to our baser natures, and superficial subjective analysis couched in objective clothing, I welcome the opportunity to challenge the racist and sexist myths that continue to survive in the minds of so many about the black woman and the black man. These myths need to be brought out so that they can be buried once and for all.

I speak for Sapphire because I am Sapphire. Black men will learn little of me from books like the *Black Man's Guide*. Books like mine are not to put down the black man, but instead to stress the point that black men are a product of their environment and conditioning just as black women are. Many black men unwittingly perpetrate sexism in the black community but from their perspective as perpetrators, find it difficult to understand the complaints of the black woman. Some, however, see but do not care. This is why black women must be ever vigilant about eliminating the oppression of black women. The future victims will be our daughters and granddaughters.

To the black men who do not understand me, let me explain. On the days when I do not smile, it is because I have little to smile about. I am not a plastic Barbie doll with no feelings who can continually smile. Neither am I one of Pavlov's dogs who can be trained to grin whenever it would make a black man feel good. For the most part, I am tired of being damned if I do and damned if I don't. I do not sit down because I am afraid to sit down. I have seen too many black women perish. Many of the black women whom I have seen perish have perished at the hands of black men. I give blind obedience to no one because all humans err. Yes, I take my life seriously because when I came close to losing my life, I realized how much I value my life.

Unlike the black woman presented in the *Black Man's Guide* who is "like the rock of the earth" and "longs to settle down," I have lived in six states, pursuing better opportunities and a better life for my son and me. My home is not where I was born or where I lived yesterday, but instead where I live today. My home is wherever I can survive. Had I sat and waited to be saved by a black knight I would have perished long ago, and my son with me. Because I have survived without a man, I am labeled Sapphire, the contentious sister from hell, and blamed for every failure of the black race by those like the *Black Man's Guide*.

I am blamed for the scourge of teen pregnancy when my own son was born six days before my twenty-fifth birthday. I am blamed for the drug scourge in the black community when the only drugs I do are aspirins and an occasional sleeping pill. I am blamed for the disproportionate number of blacks in prison when I too am victimized by institutionalized racism as well as the black men whose disproportionate numbers over fill our prisons. I confess that I am guilty of maintaining a single-parent household, but short of shooting myself and thereby effecting a no-parent household, I have no solution to my dilemma. I cannot make my son's father take an interest in our son and I know few single black men who are interested in a single woman with a child. In the years that my son was in the Big Brother program, his big brothers were all white males.

Though I know that I am not the kind of black woman in which most black men are interested, there are so many productive uses to which I can put my skills that transforming myself into a black Barbie doll so that I can catch a man is not ranked high among my priorities. My social conditioning did not take and I find legal work, yard work, electrical work, playing with my computer, or watching time fly by more fulfilling than housework. There is always a trail of books in almost every room in my household and frequently when I go to sleep, there are books in my bed. I have not owned a stereo or a television since 1979 but I always enjoy conversations with the few friends that visit, conversations that have lasted for hours on end.

Only once has my housekeeping thoroughly embarrassed me. A male visitor with whom I was quite fond of debating and I were engaged in a scorching debate. He made a grand gesture to emphasize a point, flung his arm out to his side and knocked over a pile of books that sat precariously perched on a shelf next to his seat. When the huge stack of books tumbled onto his head and covered his lap while he was in the middle of making a disagreeable statement about women, I roared with laughter. Thankfully he was not hurt because I could not stop laughing in spite of my embarrassment. He swore that I had planned the whole thing but being the argumentative type that he was he simply moved his chair and continued to debate, just as I have continued to detest housework.

Strangely, black men cannot see that I and the millions of Sapphires like me have been so busy struggling to keep our own heads above water and our children afloat that we have had little time to spend plotting against black men. So be it. With all that I have survived, I will not be defeated by a label. Though companionship is nice, I have learned to survive alone. My human dignity means more to me than sex. Though I work hard, my life is not so devoid of personal satisfaction that I will do "anything" to keep a man. I love my people and am concerned about our future, but just as I do not support the slogan "My country right or wrong," I do not support the black community, right or wrong. When my country is wrong, I have taken and will continue to take to the streets in protest. When my community is wrong, I will protest that error, too.

Though I did not ask to come here, America is my country and I will not let any white man or black man tell me otherwise. Those whites who would suggest that I go back to Africa should themselves consider going back to Europe. Those blacks who would suggest that we go back to Africa will have to leave without me. I intend to stay in America—a country that has denied my history and my humanity—and fight to the death for what is mine.

My unknown black ancestors came on slave ships en route from Africa, but my unknown white ancestors came on ships like the

Mayflower en route from European countries. Though my white ancestors do not claim me, their legacy lives on in the green-eyed, yellow-skinned blacks among my race. My ancestors lived in separate worlds, not unlike blacks and whites today. I know little of the one or two native Americans who somehow got mixed in with my great-great-grandparents in their migration to Texas.

I was privileged to meet two of my great-grandmothers when I was a child. When one of my great-grandmothers was on her death bed, we were taken to see her for the first and last time. Her old clapboard house brimmed over with those coming to pay their last respects, but the night was like a party. There were food and drinks and laughter and tail-wagging mongrel dogs who kept the cats that attempted to mingle with us at bay under the high front porch. The best places on the porch were reserved for those with canes and those in cradles. There were so many people there that we had to take turns visiting with Little Mama.

She was a very animated brown-skinned woman with colorful bed coverings, coarse white hair and many adult children. She told us stories of people we had never seen and times we had never known. There has never been another night like that night. The night air was so crisp and clear that it was impossible to tell where the black night ended and the black sky began. One could almost reach out into the darkness and touch the moon. The moon and stars hung in the black sky like the bright lights on a Christmas tree when everyone in the household has gone to bed except one curious child who creeps towards the tree in the darkness lest the others be aroused. Just as Little Mama had told us when she kissed us good-bye the night before, she did not wake up the next morning. She had seemed so alive among her colorful quilts that I did not believe she would really die that night. When I asked my dad how she knew she would die, he said that old folks just knew.

My other great-grandmother was a small, red-skinned woman with a single long white braid the length of her back. She had one lone son, my grandfather, who kept her near him throughout his life. She was neat as a pin and seldom spoke. When she did speak, she was frugal with her words. Like my grandfather, she had very high cheekbones and a keen eye. She could see everything in the room without ever turning her head. Sometimes she played an old Victrola and looked longingly at an old tin photograph. But, usually she just sat in a rocker in a corner and stared out of the window. Her cats would come only to her. She was fond of the grass and the sky.

Before her death, she had to be placed in a nursing home because she kept running away. She was determined to return to her birth place even though everyone she knew was long dead. I never understood her ways but being curious, I frequently watched her across the room.

Sometimes I would sit in her kitchen and watch her brush her long white hair that looked like corn silk. She never used a mirror. Occasionally she would smile at me. Whenever she ran away, I was always sorry to learn of her recapture. She was like a bird with clipped wings who never gave up trying to fly. I was too young to understand why they could not let her go but old enough to understand that she desperately longed for something or someone that she could not find at her house.

Some days she was so sad that I wanted to cry tears for her. She never cried. I would have traded my most precious toy for the opportunity to read her mind for one day. She had much to tell but never told it. She died shortly after she was placed in the nursing home.

My family is a hodgepodge of missing jig-saw puzzle pieces of man's inhumanity to man. Even as a child I wondered why the world was so mean to dark people. Because my roots are truncated, I know little of who I am. Nonetheless, I am proud of my multi-colored race that has been bastardized by white men. Bastards are but the innocent victims of the sins of others. There is no undoing the damage that has been done. One of my grandmothers used to tell us that we had to learn to be satisfied. As a child, I could not understand how one could learn to be satisfied when satisfaction came from the heart, not the brain. As an adult, I have learned the lesson.

I am not ashamed of what I am and offer no apology to anyone on account of my race. Likewise, I offer no apology to the black man for what I am. In spite of what many brothers may think, I support their freedom to choose the "kinder, gentler white woman." However, I will not be frightened or bullied into submission nor be kept in a woman's "place" because some black men prefer white women.

I, too, like to soar like a bird. I am not looking for security because I have learned that there is none. I have but to look at the black race to see that security is like a mirage hovering over a hot Texas highway—it comes and it goes. I am content to remain Sapphire.

I am proud of the so-called strong black women of America: a group of women whose only crime is to be able to survive without men. Having been forced to stand on my feet and having learned how to stand, I will no longer sit. I will take a back seat to no one—not the white man, the white woman, or the black man. My place is wherever I choose to sit.

I have learned to stand up for myself the hard way and stand I will. I have been knocked down so many times, I no longer fear being knocked down. Though some who are continually knocked down learn to stay down, I have learned to get back up. I am just as worthy as any other human being whether or not my country or community acknowledges me.

136

Though dying alone is the boogey man held out to every woman, I have seen enough deaths to know that death is a solitary act. Everyone dies alone, even those that die in a room crowded with people. I have not learned to be perfect because that is a lesson that cannot be taught. I have learned to be true to myself. I no longer run from battles.

I am proud to be a black woman and proud of my sisters who have broken their backs because of the love they held in their hearts for their children or men or other women and their communities. I treasure these women and acknowledge that without them I would not be here. I thank every Sapphire who ever marched, preached, and pissed somebody off so that black women with the desire may have the opportunity to learn to fly.

Unlike the new conservative blacks who now disown affirmative action, I am not so vain or conceited or absent-minded as to believe that my limited success in life has been due to my qualifications. Many much smarter than I have never gotten a foot in the door or died trying.

My grandfather, who had a Ph.D in mathematics, spoke in addition to English, Spanish, French and Latin though he had never been outside the United States. He was a genius but he could teach only at black colleges because of his black skin. He should have had a choice. He did not. He was luckier than most of the young boys he used to play with in the railroad yard near his home. Because he made himself useful at the train yard with his ability to place his ear to the ground and tell when the train was coming, and knew all the train schedules by heart, he became known to a couple of white legislators who regularly rode through the train station on their way to the state capital in Austin. In their arrogance, they could not believe that a young black boy could be that smart. My grandfather was frequently called upon to perform. To their credit, a couple of the legislators helped my great-grandmother, who was very poor, to keep my grandfather in school.

Like many black boys today, my grandfather never knew his father, who took off when he was a baby. My grandfather saw his father once when he was twelve years old. When his father came to see what he looked like, my grandfather told him to go back where he came from. My grandfather never saw his father again.

My parents also fell victim to the institutionalized racism in America. Although my father served his country as a sergeant in World War II and was subsequently able to receive a master's degree under the G.I. bill, and in spite of the fact that my father worked for the ultimate equal opportunity employer, the federal government, he generally worked for white supervisors who had only high school diplomas. Though he had more education than anyone in his department, he never rose in the ranks. He did, however, earn more than my mother, who also had a master's degree, but who had the misfortune to be a teacher in a society where those who fix cars are more valued than those who fix the minds of children.

I have had many doors slammed in my qualified or over-qualified black face, whichever was most convenient for the door slammer. In frustration, I turned to the electrical trade knowing that there I would receive at least the same union scale that the other workers received. I have had many doors opened for me by unknown and sometimes illiterate blacks who died in the struggle for the civil rights of blacks in America. Though equal opportunity remains the tasteless joke it has always been, some in my generation have managed to get a foot in the door. That is generally where we remain, with one foot hanging in the door, hoping that no one pushes against the door too hard and crushes the one foot we have managed to get in, before we can get the other foot inside. I cannot be fooled into thinking that I have equal rights by the appointment of one black Supreme Court Justice or a few black police chiefs. I have seven sisters and brothers with college degrees, none of whom have been able to get promoted like their white peers. For us, racism is not an academic experience. It is a day-to-day reality.

While I do not condone the destruction of the property of others, I thank those unknown black men and women whose last act in life was to throw a molotov cocktail through a plate glass window to get white America's attention. Whether we label these sisters and brothers guided or misguided, had they not gotten the attention of the white community, the bureaucrats in the system of mazes that swept my parents and grandparents out of the game would have swept me out into the streets also when my turn came to run the mazes, on the basis of my skin color alone.

Ironically, the same school that denied my mother admission some forty years ago (actually they offered to pay for her to go someplace else) because of the color of her skin, the University of Texas offered me admission to its law school class some forty years later. I am not so naive as to believe that my summa cum laude credentials from Fordham University opened the same door that was slammed in my mother's black face. The door was opened by the black men and women who took to the streets during the civil rights era. The door was opened by the black men and women in ghettos across America who in sheer frustration threatened to burn America to the ground during the sixties and early seventies. One could conclude that those who burned their own neighborhoods were foolish, or one could conclude that they were so angry that they would have burned anything in their paths to express their rage and total frustration, including white America. Affirmative action was a good deal for white America but as the treaties with the

Native Americans should have shown us, America is a country that strikes a bargain and then changes the rules after getting the benefit of the bargain. The rules were changed on the Native Americans in the name of manifest destiny. Now blacks are told that the rules must change to ensure a color-blind society.

Though my parents were ecstatic about my acceptance to U.T., I accepted a better offer on the West coast. My memory is not so short that I have forgotten from whence I come. Not in my wildest dream do I ever imagine that whites will accept blacks as equals. The color-blind society, like the fountain of youth, exists only in the imagination of mankind. I gave up all Quixotic fantasies long ago and have ceased to chase windmills.

I do, however, still have hope that someday the black man will give Sapphire the decent burial she deserves. I fear that as long as we insist on the natural superiority of a sex (or race) that some elite group will dominate the rest of us and monsters will be bred to hate those who are not part of the elite group. The black woman cannot win in the game of superiority because she has two strikes against her: black and female.

In spite of the fact that the black woman's experiences are made invisible by whites and black men, the black woman is forced to deal with legends that pre-date her arrival in America. Until she gains a voice of her own, the black woman is forced to tell her story in the voice of the white male— 'we," the white female— women," or the black male— 'blacks." Thus the black woman is easily drowned out. Like the legends surrounding the ghost of the yellow dog, the legends about Sapphire continue to grow and there is no rest for her weary soul. How much longer? The hateful garbage that was written about black women by a black woman in the *Black Man's Guide* is clear evidence that the voices of the white male, the white female, and the black male have been so loud that some black women have not been able to learn their own voices. This is a monumental tragedy for not only black women but America as well. Having watched one of my great-grandmothers die without telling her story, I am saddened at the prospect that the voices of legions of black women will not be heard. The black woman in America has much to tell but has yet to tell it.

The infection in our minds regarding Sapphire must be brought out into the sunlight before a healing can result. Blaming the black woman for all the problems in the black community will not make the problems evaporate. These problems, compounded by hatred and violence, will instead continue to fester and grow.

Those black men who believe that slapping black women in the mouth will keep them from complaining about the problems in their homes or communities have either not heard or have sorely misunderstood the voices of black women. If the history of slavery in America has taught us anything, it is that silence is a crime. America cannot drown out the voice of the black woman. I, for one, will no longer be silenced because I am "only" a woman.

Appendix

MEDIAN INCOME OF YEAR-ROUND FULL-TIME WORKERS			
White Male	*Black Male*	*White Female*	*Black Female*
1980 19,720	13,875	11,703	10,915
1985 25,693	17,971	16,482	14,590
1987 27,303	19,522	17,889	15,978
1988 28,262	20,716	18,823	16,867

Source: U.S. Bureau of the Census, *Current Population Reports*, series P-60, no. 162.

Notes

Chapter One
1. Ali, *The Black Man's Guide*.
2. Parsons, *How Capitalism Underdeveloped* 69.
3. Moynihan, "The Tangle of Pathology," 29.
4. Time, "Money and Race."
5. Ali, *The Black Man's Guide*, 180.
6. *Ibid.*, 179.
7. *Ibid.*, 181.
8. *Ibid.*, 110.

Chapter Two
9. Ali, *The Black Man's Guide*, 9.
10. Romero, "UCLA Student Denied Access," 3.
11. *L.A. News*.
12. Madhubuti, *Confusion by Any Other Name*.
13. Wolfgang, "Racial Discrimination," 116.
14. Ibid., 110-113.
15. LaFree, *The Effect of Sexual Stratification*, 842, 852.
16. Wriggins, *Rape, Racism and the Law*, 103.
17. Ibid., 118.
18. Amir, *Patterns in Forcible Rape*; Peters, "The Philadelphia Rape Survey."
19. Amir, *Patterns in Forcible Rape*; Hinderland & Davis, "Forcible Rape"; Karmen, "Women Victims"; Katz & Mazur, *Understanding the Rape Victim*; Peters, "Children Are Victims."
20. Karmen, *Women Victims of Crime*, 185, 188.

Chapter Three
21. Moynihan, "The Tangle of Pathology," 30.
22. Ibid., 29.
23. Ibid., 30.
24. Ibid.

25. Ibid., 34.

Chapter Four
26. For a complete discussion of matriarchy, see Hooks, *Ain't I a Woman*; Davis, "Reflections on the Black Woman's Role"; Diner, *Mothers and Amazons*.
27. Moynihan, "The Tangle of Pathology," 29.
28. Aptheker, "The Matriarchal Mirage."
29. Ibid.
30. U.S. Bureau of the Census, *Current Population Reports*, series P-60, no. 162.
31. Hooks, *Ain't I a Woman*.
32. Ibid., 92.
33. Axelson, "The Working Wife."
34. Stokes, "Black Woman to Black Man."
35. Hooks, *Ain't I a Woman*.
36. Ibid., 117.

Chapter Five
37. Freeman, "Legitimizing Racial Discrimination"; id., *Antidiscrimination Law*.
38. Freeman, "Antidiscrimination Law"; 124.
39. Crenshaw, "Race, Reform, and Retrenchment," 101.
40. Ibid., 1344.
41. Freeman, *62 Minn. L. Rev*, 1054.
42. Bell, "Property Barriers."
43. For a complete discussion of unconscious racism, which I find analogous to sex discrimination, see Lawrence, "The Id, the Ego, and Equal Protection: Reckoning with Unconscious Racism."

Chapter Six
44. Dillard, "The Emancipation Proclamation."

Chapter Seven
45. Ali, Black Man's Guide, 145.
46. Ibid., 146.

47. Ibid., 163.

48. Ibid., 155.

49. Ibid.

50. Ibid.

51. Ibid., 28.

52. Ibid., 170.

53. Ibid., 30.

54. Ibid., 132-133.

55. Ibid., 151.

56. Ibid.

57. Ibid.

58. Ibid., 152.

59. Ibid.

Chapter Eight

60. 2 Live Crew lyrics.

61. Ice Cube lyrics, *AmeriKKKa's Most Wanted*.

62. Gates, "2 Live Crew, Decoded" byline.

63. "Two Tales of The Apocalypse," 53.

64. "Marshall Retires," 1.

Bibliography

Ali, S. *The Black Man's Guide to Understanding the Black Woman*. Philadelphia: Civilized Press, 1989.

Amir, J. *Patterns in Forcible Rape*. Chicago: University of Chicago Press, 1971.

Aptheker, B. "The Matriarchal Mirage: The Moynihan Connection Historical Perspective." In *Women's Legacy: Essays on Race, Sex, and Class in American History*. Amherst: Univ. Mass. Press, 1982.

Axelson, L. J. "The Working Wife: Difference in Perception Among Negro and White Males." N.P. 1970. Cited by Hooks, B., *Ain't I a Woman*. Boston: South End Press, 1981.

Bell, D. "Property Barriers and Fair Housing Laws." In *Race, Racism and American Law*. Boston: Little, Brown & Co., 1980.

Crenshaw, K. "Race, Reform, and Retrenchment: Transformation and Legitimation in Discrimination Law." *Harv L. Rev.* 101 (1988): 1331.

Davis, A. "Reflections on the Black Woman's Role in the Community of Slaves." *The Black Scholar*, 3, no. 4 (December 1971).

Dillard. "The Emancipation Proclamation in the Perspective of Time." *Law in Transition* 23 (1963): 95.

Diner, H. *Mothers and Amazons*. New York: Anchor Press, 1973.

Freeman, A. "Legitimizing Racial Discrimination through Antidiscrimination Law: A Critical Review of Supreme Court Doctrine." *Minn L. Rev.* 62 (1978): 1049.

————. "Antidiscrimination Law: The View from 1989." In *The Politics of Law*. 2d ed. N.Y.: Pantheon Books, 1990.

Hinderland, M. J. & B. L. Davis. "Forcible Rape in the United States: A Statistical Profile." In *Forcible Rape: The Crime, the Victim and the Offender*, edited by D. Chappell, P. Geis, & G. Geis, 87-114. New York: Columbia Univ. Press, 1977.

Hooks, B. *Ain't I a Woman*. Boston: South End Press, 1981.

Ice Cube. AmeriKKKa's Most Wanted © 1989.

Karmen. "Women Victims of Crime: Introduction." In *The Criminal Justice System and Women: Offenders, Victims, Workers*, edited by B. Price & N. Sololoff, 185, 188. N.Y.: Clark Boardman, 1982.

Katz, S. & M. A. Mazur. *Understanding the Rape Victim: A Synthesis of Research Findings*. New York: Wiley, 1979.

LaFree. "The Effect of Sexual Stratification by Race on Official Reactions to Rape." *Amer. Soc. Rev.* 45 (1980): 842, 852.

Lawrence, C. "The Id, the Ego, and Equal Protection: Reckoning with Unconscious Racism." *Stanford L. Rev.* 39 (1987): 317.

Madhubuti, H., et al. *Confusion by Any Other Name: Essays Exploring the Negative Impact of "The Black man's Guide to Understanding the Black woman."* Chicago: Third World Press, 1990.

"Marshall Retires From High Court; Blow to Liberals." *New York Times*, 28 June 1991: 1.

Miller, J. et al., "Recidivism Among Sexual Assault Victims." *American Journal of Psychiatry* 135 (1978): 1103-1104; U.S. Dept. of Justice, Law Enforcement Assistance Administration, National Criminal Justice Information, and Statistics Service, Washington, D.C., *National Crime Panel Survey Report: Criminal Victimization Surveys in the Nation's Five Largest Cities*: Government Printing Office, 1975.

"Money and Race." *Time* (December 1989): Personal Finance Section.

Moynihan, D. "The Tangle of Pathology." In *The Negro Family—A Case for National Action*, 29-30. Washington: Office of Policy Planning & Research, U.S. Dept. of Labor, 1965.

Parsons, Lucy. Quoted in Marable, M., *How Capitalism Underdeveloped Black America*, 69. Boston: South End Press, 1983.

Peters, J. J. "Children Are Victims of Sexual Assault and the Psychology of Offenders." *American Journal of Psychotherapy* 30 (1976): 393-421.

Peters. "The Philadelphia Rape Survey." In *Victimology: A New Focus*, Vol. III, Crimes, Victims and Justice, 186. Lexington: Lexington Books, 1975.

Rainwater, L. & W. Yancey, *The Moynihan Report & The Politics of Controversy*. Cambridge: The M.I.T. Press, 1967.

Romero, Dennis. "UCLA Student Denied Access to Jewelry Store." *Daily Bruin News*, 7 June 1990, 3.

Stokes, G. "Black Woman to Black Man." In *The Liberator*, 1968. Cited by Hooks, B. *Ain't I A Woman*, 92-93. Boston: South End Press, 1981.

"2 Live Crew, Decoded." *New York Times*, 19 June 1990, late ed. sec. A: 23. (Byline by Henry Louis Gates Jr., Professor of English at Duke University).

"Two Tales of the Apocalypse: A Novel of Incest Mirrors an Author's Pain." *Newsweek* 15 (July 1991): 53.

U.S. Bureau of the Census, *Current Population Reports*, series P–60, no. 162, and unpublished data.

Wolfgang. "Racial Discrimination in the Death Sentence for Rape." In *Executions in America*, 116. Lexington: Lexington Books.

Wriggins, J. "Rape, Racism, and the Law." *Harv. Women's L.J.* (1983): 103.